Gooney Bird Greene
3 Books in 1!

Read all the
Gooney Bird Greene books!

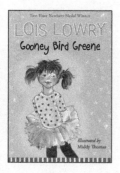

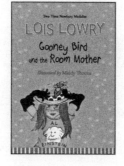

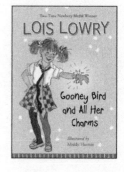

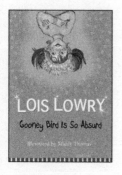

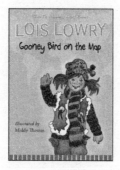

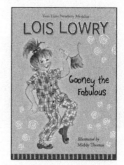

Gooney Bird Greene
3 Books in 1!

Gooney Bird Greene

Gooney Bird and the Room Mother

Gooney the Fabulous

LOIS LOWRY

Illustrated by Middy Thomas

HOUGHTON MIFFLIN HARCOURT
Boston New York

For information about permission to reproduce selections from
this book, write to trade.permissions@hmhco.com or to Permissions,
Houghton Mifflin Harcourt Publishing Company, 3 Park Avenue,
19th Floor, New York, New York 10016.

www.hmhco.com

The text of this book is set in Garamond MT.

Library of Congress Cataloging-in-Publication Data
for individual titles is on file.

ISBN: 978-0-544-84824-5

Manufactured in the United States of America
DOC 10 9 8 7 6 5 4 3 2 1
4500588069

Gooney Bird Greene

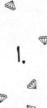

1.

There was a new student in the Watertower Elementary School. She arrived in October, after the first month of school had already passed. She opened the second grade classroom door at ten o'clock on a Wednesday morning and appeared there all alone, without even a mother to introduce her. She was wearing pajamas and cowboy boots and was holding a dictionary and a lunch box.

"Hello," Mrs. Pidgeon, the second grade teacher, said. "We're in the middle of our spelling lesson."

"Good," said the girl in pajamas. "I brought my dictionary. Where's my desk?"

"Who are you?" Mrs. Pidgeon asked politely.

"I'm your new student. My name is Gooney Bird Greene — that's Greene with a silent 'e' at the end — and I just moved here from China. I want a desk right smack in the middle of the room, because I like to be right smack in the middle of everything."

The class stared at the new girl with admiration. They had never met anyone like Gooney Bird Greene.

She was a good student. She sat down at the desk Mrs. Pidgeon provided, right smack in the middle of everything, and began doing second grade spelling. She did all her work neatly and quickly, and she followed instructions.

But soon it was clear that Gooney Bird was mysterious and interesting. Her clothes were unusual. Her hairstyles were unusual. Even her lunches were very unusual.

At lunchtime on Wednesday, her first day in the school, she opened her lunch box and brought out sushi and a pair of bright green chopsticks. On Thursday, her second day at Watertower Elementary School, Gooney Bird Greene was wearing a pink ballet tutu over green stretch pants, and she had three small red grapes, an avocado, and an oatmeal cookie for lunch.

On Thursday afternoon, after lunch, Mrs. Pidgeon stood in front of the class with a piece of chalk in her hand. "Today," she said, "we are going to continue talking about stories."

"Yay!" the second-graders said in very loud voices, all but Felicia Ann, who never spoke, and Malcolm, who wasn't paying attention. He was under his desk, as usual.

"Gooney Bird, you weren't here for the first month of school. But our class has been learning about what makes good stories, haven't we?" Mrs. Pidgeon said. Everyone nodded. All but Malcolm, who was under his desk doing something with scissors.

"Class? What does a story need most of all? Who remembers?" Mrs. Pidgeon had her chalk hand in the air, ready to write something on the board.

The children were silent for a minute. They were thinking. Finally Chelsea raised her hand.

"Chelsea? What does a story need?"

"A book," Chelsea said.

Mrs. Pidgeon put her chalk hand down. "There are many stories that don't need a book," she said pleasantly, "aren't there, class? If your grandma tells you a story about when she was a little girl, she doesn't have that story in a book, does she?"

The class stared at her. All but Malcolm, who was still under his desk, and Felicia Ann, who always looked at the floor, never raised her hand, and never spoke.

Beanie said, "My grandma lives in Boston!"

Keiko said, "My grandma lives in Honolulu!"

Ben said loudly, "My grandma lives in Harrisburg, Pennsylvania!"

Tricia shouted, "My grandma is very rich!"

"Class!" said Mrs. Pidgeon. "Shhh!" Then, in a quieter voice, she explained, "Another time, we will talk about our families. But right now —" She stopped talking and looked at Barry Tuckerman. Barry was up on his knees in his seat, and his hand was waving in the air as hard as he could make it wave.

"Barry?" Mrs. Pidgeon said. "Do you have something that you simply have to say? Something that cannot possibly wait?"

Barry nodded yes. His hand waved.

"And what is so important?"

Barry stood up beside his desk. Barry Tuckerman liked to make very important speeches, and they always required that he stand.

"My grandma," Barry Tuckerman said, "went to jail once. She was twenty years old and she went to jail for civil disobedience." Then Barry sat down.

"Thank you, Barry. Now look at what I'm writing on the board. Who can read this word?"

Everyone, all but Malcolm and Felicia Ann, watched as she wrote the long word. Then they shouted it out. "BEGINNING!"

"Good!" said Mrs. Pidgeon. "Now I'm sure you'll all know this one." She wrote again.

"MIDDLE!" the children shouted.

"Good. And can you guess what the last word will be?" She held up her chalk and waited.

"END!"

"Correct!" Mrs. Pidgeon said. "Good for you, second-graders! Those are the parts that a story needs: a beginning, a middle, and an end. Now I'm going to write another very long word on the board. Let's see what good readers you are." She wrote a C, then an H.

"Mrs. Pidgeon!" someone called.

She wrote an A, and then an R.

"MRS. PIDGEON!" Several children were calling now.

She turned to see what was so important. Malcolm was standing beside his desk. He was crying.

"Malcolm needs to go to the nurse, Mrs. Pidgeon!" Beanie said.

Mrs. Pidgeon went to Malcolm and knelt beside him. "What's the trouble, Malcolm?" she asked. But he couldn't stop crying.

"I know, I know!" Nicholas said. Nicholas always knew everything, and his desk was beside Malcolm's.

"Tell me, Nicholas."

"Remember Keiko showed us how to make origami stars?"

All of the second-graders reached into their desks and their pockets and their lunch boxes. There were tiny stars everywhere. Keiko had shown them how to make origami stars out of small strips of paper. The stars were very easy to make. The school janitor had complained just last Friday that he was sweeping up hundreds of origami stars.

"Malcolm put one in his nose," Nicholas said, "and now he can't get it out."

"Is that correct, Malcolm?" Mrs. Pidgeon asked. Malcolm nodded and wiped his eyes.

"Don't sniff, Malcolm. *Do not sniff.* That is an order." She took his hand and walked with him to the classroom door. She turned to the class. "Children," she said, "I am going to be gone for exactly one minute and thirty seconds while I walk with Malcolm to the nurse's office down the hall. Stay in your seats while I'm gone. Think about the word *character.*

"A character is what a story needs. When I come back from the nurse's office, we are going to create a story together. You must choose who the main character will be. Talk among yourselves quietly. Think about interesting

characters like Abraham Lincoln, or perhaps Christopher Columbus, or —"

"Babe Ruth?" called Ben.

"Yes, Babe Ruth is a possibility. I'll be right back."

Mrs. Pidgeon left the classroom with Malcolm.

When she returned, one minute and thirty seconds later, without Malcolm, the class was waiting. They had been whispering, all but Felicia Ann, who never whispered.

"Have you chosen?" she asked. The class nodded. All of their heads went up and down, except Felicia Ann's, because she always looked at the floor.

"And your choice is —?"

All of the children, all but Felicia Ann, called out together. "Gooney Bird Greene!" they called.

Mrs. Pidgeon sighed. "Class," she said, "there are many different kinds of stories. There are stories about imaginary creatures, like —"

"Dumbo!" Tricia called out.

"Raise your hand if you want to speak, please," Mrs. Pidgeon said. "But yes, Tricia, you are correct. Dumbo is an imaginary character. There are also stories about real people from history, like Christopher Columbus, and —" She stopped. Barry Tuckerman was waving and waving his hand. "Yes, Barry? Do you have something very important to say?"

Barry Tuckerman stood up. He twisted the bottom of his shirt around and around in his fingers. "I forget," he said at last.

"Well, sit back down then, Barry. Now, I thought, class, that since Christopher Columbus's birthday is coming up soon —" She looked at Barry Tuckerman, whose hand was waving like a windmill once again. "Barry?" she said.

Barry Tuckerman stood up again. "We already know all the stories about Christopher Columbus," he said. "We want to hear a true story about Gooney Bird Greene."

"Yes! Gooney Bird Greene!" the class called.

Mrs. Pidgeon sighed again. "I'm afraid I don't know many facts abut Gooney Bird Greene," she said. "I know a *lot* of facts about Christopher Columbus, though. Christopher Columbus was born in —"

"We want Gooney Bird!" the class chanted.

"Gooney Bird?" Mrs. Pidgeon said, finally. "How do you feel about this?"

Gooney Bird Greene stood up beside her desk in the middle of the room. "Can I tell the story?" she asked. "Can I be right smack in the middle of everything? Can I be the hero?"

"Well, since you would be the main character," Mrs. Pidgeon said, "I guess that would put you in the middle of everything. I guess that would make you the hero."

"Good," Gooney Bird said. "I will tell you an absolutely true story about me."

2.

Gooney Bird adjusted the pink ballet tutu she was wearing over a pair of green stretch pants. Her T-shirt was decorated with polka dots. Her red hair was pulled into two pigtails and held there with blue scrunchies.

She pulled carefully on one of her pigtails, rearranging it neatly, because the scrunchie was coming loose. She felt her earlobes, which were small and pink and empty.

"I should have worn the dangling diamond earrings that I got from the prince," she told the class. "Maybe I'll wear them next week."

"Diamond earrings? Prince?" Mrs. Pidgeon asked.

"Well, actually, the prince didn't give me the earrings. I got them at the palace," Gooney Bird explained.

"Why were you at the palace?"

"Well, first I was in jail, and then —" Gooney Bird interrupted herself. "It's a long story." She reached down and tidied her socks.

"May I come up to the front of the room to begin?" she asked the teacher after she had adjusted her clothes. "I like to be absolutely the center of attention."

Mrs. Pidgeon nodded and stepped aside so that there was room for Gooney Bird to stand in the front of the class.

"You might as well sit down, Mrs. Pidgeon," Gooney Bird said politely. "Take a load off your feet."

Mrs. Pidgeon sat down in the chair behind her cluttered desk. She looked at the clock on the wall. "We have fifteen minutes," she said, "before arithmetic."

"Class," Gooney Bird said, "you heard Mrs. Pidgeon. We have just fifteen minutes. There are many Gooney Bird stories I might tell you, but I have time for only one today. Who has a suggestion for a story?"

Ben's hand shot up. "Tell about how you came from China," he said.

Nicholas called, "Why are you named Gooney Bird?"

Chelsea was wiggling and wiggling in her seat. "The palace!" she said. "Tell about jail, and the palace, and the diamond earrings!"

Other hands were waving, but Gooney Bird motioned for those children to put their hands down. She looked around the room, thinking.

"This is the title of the story," she said at last. "'How Gooney Bird Got Her Name.'"

"Just like *How the Leopard Got His Spots,*" Barry Tuckerman said in a loud whisper.

"Barry, pay attention, please," Gooney Bird said. "I like to have absolutely all eyes on me."

Then, when the class was silent, and all eyes, except those of Felicia Ann, who always looked at the floor, were on her, she began.

How Gooney Bird Got Her Name

Once upon a time, eight years ago, a man and a woman named Mr. and Mrs. Greene — that's Greene with a silent 'e' at the end — discovered that they were expecting a baby girl.

The man's name was Gordon Greene. His wife was Barbara Greene.

They decided to name their baby girl with their initials. G for Gordon, B for Barbara.

They thought of many different names.

"Gail Beth," said Mrs. Greene. She liked short names.

"Gwendolyn Belinda," said Mr. Greene. He liked long names.

They discussed and discussed. They never argued or fought. But they had many discussions.

Once, in the middle of the night, Mrs. Greene woke up. She had had a dream about a name. She nudged Mr. Greene until he woke up a little bit. Then she said, "Georgina Babette."

"No," he said, and went back to sleep.

One night Mr. Greene woke up, nudged his wife, and told her that he had had a dream. "Gazpacho Banana," he said.

"That was a nightmare you had," his wife said. He agreed. They both went back to sleep.

Finally, because they could not make up their minds about a name, they decided that they would wait until the baby girl was born. Then they would look at the baby and somehow they would know that her name should be Grace Bridget, or Gloria Bonnie, or some other name.

They waited and waited for the baby's birth. It takes many months, as you know.

Gooney Bird paused in her story. She could see that many of the children wanted to wave their hands in the air and say things.

"Class?" she said. "Any comments so far? Any questions?"

"We have nine minutes left," Mrs. Pidgeon reminded them, "before arithmetic."

Keiko asked in a small voice, "Did he really say Gazpacho Banana?"

"Yes, he did," Gooney Bird said. "I tell only absolutely true stories."

Barry Tuckerman stood up beside his desk. "I was named a B name for my grandfather," he said. "My grandfather's name was Benjamin."

"That's *my* name!" Ben called out.

"My grandfather was in college when my grandmother went to jail," Barry added, "or he would have gone with her."

Tricia raised her hand. "My cat's name is Fluffernutter," she said.

"Four more minutes!" Mrs. Pidgeon announced. "Let's let Gooney Bird get back to her story so that we can hear the ending.

"Did you notice, class," she added, "how she uses *characters* and *dialogue*? And her story is full of suspense. It's a cliffhanger, isn't it? What a good storyteller Gooney Bird is!"

"Ready?" Gooney Bird asked.

"Ready!" shouted the class, all but Felicia Ann, who never shouted.

"Okay. Here comes the ending."

Finally, one spring morning, the baby girl was born. She weighed six pounds and fourteen ounces. She had red hair.

"Look!" said her mother. "She wiggles

her head around, looking for food when she's hungry. Isn't that cute! It reminds me of something, but I forget what."

Her father peered down at the new baby in his wife's arms. He smiled. "She has very big feet! Isn't that cute! It reminds me of something, but I forget what."

Mr. and Mrs. Greene looked at their sweet baby. They thought and thought.

"It's coming back to me," Mr. Greene said at last. "Do you remember when we went on that bird-watching trip to various islands in the Pacific Ocean, and we saw all kinds of marine birds?"

"That's it!" his wife said. "She looks very much like one of those birds. But which one?"

"Let's get our photograph album from that trip," Mr. Greene said.

Together they turned the pages of the album.

"Double-crested cormorant?" Mrs. Greene said. They looked down at the baby. No. She didn't look like a double-crested cormorant.

"Red-necked grebe?" Mr. Greene suggested. They looked at the baby again.

"She *does* have a red neck," Mr. Greene said.

"She does not!" said Mrs. Greene. "It's pink."

They turned the pages some more. Suddenly they both said, "Oh!"

Very carefully they looked at the photograph. Then very carefully they looked at the baby.

"Big feet," Mr. Greene said. "Just like our baby's."

"A head that bobs around," Mrs. Greene said. "Just like our baby's."

"That's the one," they agreed.

They read the label under the photograph. "Laysan Albatross," the label said.

"I don't think Laysan Albatross Greene is a very pretty name for a baby girl," Mrs. Greene said sadly. "It sounds too scientific."

"I agree," Mr. Greene said. "But look at the small print."

Together Mr. and Mrs. Greene read the words in the small print: OFTEN CALLED GOONEY BIRD.

"Gooney Bird Greene!" they said.

"I like the sound of it!" Mrs. Greene said. "And it has a G and a B."

"It does indeed," said Mr. Greene.

So they decided to name their new baby girl Gooney Bird Greene. Then everyone, including a doctor, a midwife, and a cleaning lady, hugged and kissed and did a Viennese waltz together.

The End

"What a lovely story!" Mrs. Pidgeon said. "And it gives us a chance do some science research. We will look up 'Laysan Albatross' in the encyclopedia. Thank you, Gooney Bird. You may take your seat now, and we'll turn to our arithmetic."

"Wait! Wait!" Beanie's hand was waving in the air.

"Yes, Beanie?" Mrs. Pidgeon asked. "What's wrong?"

"I want to hear about the diamond earrings, and the palace!"

"That's a different story," Gooney Bird said. She was walking back to her desk.

"Tell it! Tell it!" the children called.

Barry Tuckerman jumped up and stood beside his desk. "I want to hear how Gooney Bird came from China!" he said.

"I came on a flying carpet," Gooney Bird said. "But that's a different story, too." She adjusted her pink tutu and sat down.

"Tell it! Tell it!" the children called.

Mrs. Pidgeon laughed. "I'm sure Gooney Bird was just joking about the prince and the palace and the diamond earrings," she said, "and the flying carpet, too."

Gooney Bird had already opened her arithmetic book. She looked up in surprise. "No," she said. "I wasn't joking. I tell only absolutely true stories."

"Well," said Mrs. Pidgeon, "will you tell us another tomorrow?"

"Of course," Gooney Bird said.

3.

On Friday, Gooney Bird was wearing Capri pants, a satin tank top, and a long string of pearls. Her red hair was twisted into one long braid, which was decorated with plastic flowers. There were flip-flops on her feet.

"You look beautiful," Keiko said to Gooney Bird in an admiring whisper.

"Yes, I know," Gooney Bird replied. "Thank you, Keiko." She walked to the front of the classroom when Mrs. Pidgeon told her it was time.

Malcolm was back in the classroom. He was at his desk, writing "I will never put anything

in my nose" one hundred times on a piece of lined paper. The nurse had told him to do that. She said it would keep his hands busy.

"How come Gooney Bird gets to go stand in front of the class?" Malcolm asked.

"Shhhhh," everybody, except Felicia Ann, said to Malcom. *"Listen."*

"Today," Gooney Bird said, "I have a very exciting story to tell you. In my story there is a long journey, a mystery, and a rescue."

Mrs. Pidgeon, seated at her desk, had begun correcting some spelling papers. She looked up. "Listen, second-graders," she said. "Hear the different things that Gooney Bird is putting into her story? That is what good storytellers do."

Gooney Bird listened patiently to the teacher. Then she stood up straight and did some breathing exercises. Finally she took a deep breath and looked at the class. "I am ready to begin," she said at last. "The title of the story for today will be 'How Gooney Bird Came from China on a Flying Carpet.'"

"Just like Aladdin," Barry Tuckerman said in a loud whisper.

"Barry, pay attention, please," Gooney Bird said. "I like to have absolutely all eyes on me." Then, when the class became silent — all except Felicia Ann, who had been silent all along — and almost all eyes, even Mrs. Pidgeon's, were on her, she began.

How Gooney Bird Came from China on a Flying Carpet

Once upon a time, just last month, Mr. and Mrs. Greene decided to take their little girl, Gooney Bird, and move away from the place where they had always lived.

They had always lived in China. But now Mr. Greene had a new job, and his new job was in Watertower.

"That's here!" Chelsea said aloud. "*I* live in Watertower!"

Gooney Bird stopped talking. She arranged her pearl necklace so that it was draped over one shoulder.

"Me too!" Tricia said.

"We *all* live in Watertower!" Ben pointed out. "That's why we go to the Watertower Elementary School."

"Class —" Mrs. Pidgeon warned.

"Mrs. Pidgeon," Gooney Bird said politely, "let me take care of this.

"Children," she said in a firm voice, "I cannot tell a story if I am constantly interrupted. There will be time for questions and comments. Please raise your hand if you want to say something. It's very distracting for me if you call out."

"Sorry," Tricia said.

"Sorry," Chelsea said.

"Sorry," Ben added.

The class waited. Gooney Bird looked at them all sternly. Then she did some breathing exercises and began again.

They had always lived in China. But now Mr. Greene had a new job, and his new job was in Watertower.

So they packed carefully. It took many days. First Mr. Greene had to pack forty-three sets of false teeth. Then Mrs. Greene had to pack her dancing shoes and her bathing suits. And Gooney Bird had to pack all of her belongings, which included a money collection.

Finally their furniture was loaded onto a moving van, and the Greene family waved goodbye as the moving van drove away from China and started its journey to Watertower.

Gooney Bird stopped. Every child in the classroom had a hand raised. And even Mrs. Pidgeon was waving her arm.

"I'll have an intermission now, for questions," Gooney Bird said. "Chelsea? Yours first."

"Why did Mr. Greene have forty-three pairs of false teeth?" Chelsea asked.

"The false teeth are not part of this story," Gooney Bird said. "Malcolm?"

Malcolm had looked up from his "I will not put anything in my nose" paper. His eyes were very wide. "Tell about the money collection!" he said.

"That's another story," Gooney Bird said. "Beanie?"

"When are you going to tell about the prince and the diamonds?" Beanie asked.

Gooney Bird thought it over. "On Monday I'll tell it," she said. "Now, there's time for one more question before I continue. Mrs. Pidgeon? Did you have your hand raised?"

Mrs. Pidgeon nodded. "Gooney Bird," she said in a nice voice, "you have an amazing imagination and we think you are wonderful at telling stories. Don't we, class?" She looked around, and almost all of the children nodded.

"But I want to be certain that the children understand that these are made-up stories. So I want to point out —"

"My stories are all absolutely true," Gooney Bird said.

"I want to point out," Mrs. Pidegon went on, "that of course we all know that China is a foreign country across the ocean, and that a moving van could never drive from China to Watertower."

Gooney Bird rearranged her pearls and sighed. "Mrs. Pidgeon," she said, "why don't we take a few minutes for research? Is there an atlas in the bookcase?"

Mrs. Pidgeon laughed and said, "Of course." She went to the bookcase and took out a book of maps called an atlas.

"Now," said Gooney Bird, "would you find out if there are *other* Chinas?"

"Other Chinas? I don't think —" Mrs. Pidgeon began turning the pages of the atlas. She found the index at the back.

"My goodness!" Mrs. Pidgeon said after a minute. "There's a China in Texas!"

"Correct," said Gooney Bird. "And? What else?"

"There's a China in Maine!"

"Correct," said Gooney Bird. "And?"

"California! There's a China *Lake!* Oh, and my goodness, look! In North Carolina —"

"And now it is time to continue the story," Gooney Bird announced. "Where were we? Oh, yes. I remember. The moving van had just left China —"

She took up the story again.

After the moving van left China, the Greene family loaded up their station wagon with five big suitcases. Then they added a lawn mower that they had forgotten to put in the moving van, a cooler full of ham sandwiches and iced tea, a bundled-up stack of *National Geographic*s, and an orange and white cat named Catman, who had no tail because he had flicked his former tail once under the lawn mower. The last thing they put into the station wagon was a rolled-up rug from the front porch of their house. It was too long to fit. They tried it sideways, and folded, and upside down, but it still wouldn't fit.

"Let's leave it behind," Mr. Greene suggested.

But Mrs. Greene began to cry. "It was my mother's," she said. "There's a stain on it where my mother spilled some black bean soup forty years ago. I feel sentimental about this rug."

So Mr. Greene agreed to take the rug because it made him cry, too, if his wife cried. He decided to put the back window of the station wagon down so that the end of the rolled-up rug could stick out. He made certain that everything was nicely arranged and that Catman had a comfortable place to sleep on the back seat, just beneath the end of the rug and next to the place where Gooney Bird would sit.

Mr. Greene and Mrs. Greene and Gooney Bird Greene all got into the car and drove away from China, starting their long journey to Watertower.

They drove for many, many hours. They ate all of the ham sandwiches and drank all of the iced tea. They stopped to get gas. They went to the bathroom. They played the car radio and listened to news and operas and football games and talk shows about love relationships.

Suddenly Gooney Bird glanced down and noticed with dismay that her beloved Catman had disappeared. She looked around the floor of the back seat, but Catman was not there.

She heard a small sound, like a purr, coming from inside the rolled-up rug.

She knew that Catman had entered the rug. He probably found it a warm and dark and cozy place.

But Gooney Bird was worried about Catman. She decided to try to get him out. She reached into the rolled-up center of the rug. But he slithered away, beyond her hands.

She looked at the backs of her parents' heads, wondering if she should tell them about the problem with Catman. But her mother was dozing and her father was driving, watching the road carefully and listening to a radio program about whales.

So Gooney Bird decided to wiggle into the rug herself to rescue Catman.

"Oh, no!" Keiko cried. "I'm going to faint!"
"Shhhh," the other children said.

It was dark and dusty and a very

tight squeeze inside the rolled-up rug. But Gooney Bird wiggled inch by inch toward Catman.

Catman slithered away, inch by inch. She could see his glittering eyes as he backed away from her hands. Gooney Bird was determined to rescue him. She continued forward.

Suddenly an amazing thing happened. Even though Gooney Bird was not very large and did not weigh very much — and was not wearing her heavy diamond earrings from the palace that day — her weight inside the rolled-up rug caused it to tilt. At that moment, Mr. Greene leaned forward to change the radio station, and the car went over a pothole in the road. The rolled-up rug, containing both Catman and Gooney Bird, slid out of the back of the station wagon and flew through the air before it landed at the side of the road

41

in some thick grass beside a fence post. A cow chewing a purple flower looked curiously at it and then wandered away.

The station wagon drove on, around a curve in the road. Slowly the rug unrolled. Catman's fur was standing on end, and if he had had a tail, his tail would have been sticking straight up in the air. For a moment Catman stood still, looking at Gooney Bird. Then he ran away, very fast.

Gooney Bird sat up. She was not entirely sure what had happened. But she was not hurt. She simply wondered where her family was, and her cat, and the car.

Other cars stopped and people got out. Many people offered her a drink of water from their bottles of Evian. But Gooney Bird wasn't thirsty. After a while, a police car with a flashing light came. A TV reporter came, and a cameraman. While the policeman talked on his radio, the TV reporter, a woman with very large hair, interviewed Gooney Bird and called her "the little girl who had a flying carpet ride." In the interview, Gooney Bird described Catman and asked people to call the station if they found him. But she never got Catman back.

Eventually the police car took her to her parents, who were both crying at a gas station four miles down the road.

When Gooney Bird and her parents were finally reunited, everyone, including two policemen, a TV reporter, and the gas station owner, hugged and kissed and did the tango.

The End

"What a lovely story!" Mrs. Pidgeon said. "And an exciting one, too! But a little sad, to lose your kitty that way."

"Catman is not a kitty," Gooney Bird said. "He is a cat. And I didn't say that I lost him. I just said that I never got him back."

"So no one found him and called the TV station?"

"Actually, they did," Gooney Bird replied.

"But where is Catman now?" asked Mrs. Pidgeon.

"He was consumed by a cow," Gooney Bird said, "but that's a different story."

"By a cow? You're joking," Mrs. Pidgeon said.

"No," said Gooney Bird. "I'm not joking. I tell only absolutely true stories."

"Tell it! Tell it!" the children called.

"I will," Gooney Bird said. "Another day."

4.

On Monday, Gooney Bird stood in front of the class when Mrs. Pidgeon told her that it was story time. The children barely noticed Gooney Bird's clothes, even though she was wearing a ruffled pinafore, dark blue knee socks, and high-top basketball sneakers. The second-graders, and Mrs. Pidgeon, too, were all much more interested in Gooney Bird's earrings.

The earrings dangled and glittered and were very large.

"They're beautiful," Keiko said in an awed voice.

"My grandma's house has doorknobs that

look like that," Tricia announced. "And she has a sparkly chandelier in the dining room. My grandma is very rich."

"Do you have holes in your ears?" Malcolm asked. "My mom does. My mom went and had holes stabbed right into her ears with a needle!"

"I did, too!" Beanie called out. "I have pierced ears!"

"So do I," Mrs. Pidgeon told the class. She turned her head from side to side so that they could all see her small gold earrings.

"No," Gooney Bird said. "My earrings screw onto my ears. They have little screws that you turn."

Barry Tuckerman thrust his arm into the air and waved it wildly. Around him, other children had their hands raised, too.

"My mom has pierced ears!" Barry said loudly.

"Ben?" Mrs. Pidgeon said next.

Ben said, "My mom has pierced ears and so does my grandma!"

"All right, class," Mrs. Pidgeon said. "Does anyone else have something to say which is *not* about pierced ears? Because it is time for Gooney Bird to begin today's story."

All of the hands disappeared except one. Chelsea kept her hand high in the air.

Mrs. Pidgeon sighed. "Chelsea?"

"My mom has a pierced *nose*," Chelsea told the class.

"Oh, no!" Keiko wailed. "I'm going to be sick!"

"Shhhh," the other children said.

When the class was quiet, Gooney Bird began her Monday story.

The Prince, the Palace, and
the Diamond Earrings

Once upon a time, before she moved to Watertower, when she still lived in China, Gooney Bird Greene was on her front porch, playing Monopoly against herself. Gooney Bird #1, the thimble, owned all four railroads and St. Charles Place, which she liked because it was magenta.

Gooney Bird #2, the car, was having a harder time of it. She owned Atlantic Avenue and Pennsylvania Avenue, and she liked the combination of yellow and green; she also owned both Water Works and the Electric Company, but unfortunately she was in jail.

Suddenly, just as Gooney Bird #2 tried unsuccessfully for the second time to throw doubles and get out of jail, she heard someone calling loudly, "Napoleon is missing!"

It was the prince, who lived next door.

Hands flew up into the air, and Gooney Bird looked impatiently at her classmates.

"Are these really, *really* important questions?" she asked. "Because I have just barely started the story!"

One by one most of the hands went back down.

Mrs. Pidgeon had picked up the encyclopedia. "Gooney Bird," Mrs. Pidgeon said, "I have a feeling you know this already, but Napoleon Bonaparte —" She turned to the class. "He was the emperor of France," she explained.

"Ooooh," Keiko said. "I love emperors."

Mrs. Pidgeon, still looking at the encyclopedia, went on. "Napoleon was born in 1769. That's more than two hundred years ago."

"Mrs. Pidgeon! Mrs. Pidgeon!" Barry Tuckerman was halfway out of his seat, waving his hand.

"Yes, Barry?"

"My grandmother once saw an emperor butterfly! But now it's extinct! It was purple," Barry Tuckerman said.

Gooney Bird sighed. "Do you want to hear this story or not?" she asked. "I can't wear these earrings all day. They're very heavy."

"Yes, we do," Mrs. Pidgeon said. "Please go on."

"Ready?" Gooney Bird asked the class.

Everyone was ready, so Gooney Bird continued.

"Gooney Bird," the prince called, sounding very distressed, "Napoleon has disappeared! Can you help us find him?"

Gooney Bird carefully tucked all of the Monopoly money under the edge of the board so that it wouldn't blow away. There was a slight breeze. She had had problems with money blowing away in the past. She kept her own money collection, which she carried with her at all times, safely contained in a Ziploc bag.

Then Gooney Bird set out to look for clues that might reveal the whereabouts of Napoleon.

Napoleon was not the emperor of France. He was a large black poodle.

Every hand in the second grade classroom shot up, even Felicia Ann's.

"I *knew* that would happen," Gooney Bird said. "I just knew it. Time for an intermission. Mrs. Pidgeon, do you want to deal with this?"

Mrs. Pidgeon nodded. She thought for a moment. Then she announced, "Every child who has a poodle, put your hand down."

Four hands went down.

"Now," Mrs. Pidgeon said, "every child whose grandmother has a poodle? Hands down."

Seven more hands were lowered.

"Every child who knows a poodle who does interesting tricks, or who gets into trouble, or who ran away once? Hands down."

Other hands went down, and now there were just three hands still in the air.

"Beanie? What kind of dog do you have?" Mrs. Pidgeon asked.

"Golden retriever."

"That's lovely. Ben?"

"Corgi."

"Good. And finally, Tricia?"

"I don't have a dog," Tricia said sadly. "I'm allergic to dogs. And my mother said I can never, ever have one, or even a cat, not *ever*, because I might have a terrible asthma attack, and then I would have to go to the hospital, maybe in an ambulance, and —"

"We understand, Tricia. And now let's go back to the story, because we *still* don't know what happened to Napoleon, or —"

"Or about the palace!" said Keiko. "And the earrings!"

Gooney Bird shook her head a little so that the earrings moved and sparkled in a glamorous way.

"Listen for the word *suddenly*," Gooney Bird

advised. "I put one in the story already, but I like to sprinkle in several. Some other *suddenly*s will be coming soon."

Gooney Bird examined the prince's back yard. She saw a place where the ground was disturbed by the corner of the fence.

"Look," she said. "See this bit of dog hair caught in the fence? That looks like Napoleon's.

"See?" she said next, pointing to some newly dug earth. "Here is where Napoleon wiggled under the fence."

"What a good detective you are," the prince said to Gooney Bird.

Gooney Bird let herself out of the yard and through the gate. She sniffed. She listened.

Suddenly —

"There's a *suddenly*!" called Malcolm.

"Good listening," Gooney Bird said. Then she continued.

Suddenly, because of the clues that she smelled and heard, Gooney Bird moved forward. There, at the end of the alley, was an overturned garbage can. And there, with his head inside the can, was Napoleon, eating garbage. He had coffee grounds all over his face, and an orange peel was stuck on one of his ears.

"You naughty thing, Napoleon," Gooney Bird said, and she took hold of his collar. Napoleon burped.

"Oh, no!" Keiko cried. "Not *garbage!* Not *burping!*"

"Shhhh," the other children said. Many hands were waving in the air.

Mrs. Pidgeon stood up. "No stories about

dogs eating garbage," she said firmly. "Not a single one."

All of the hands went down.

"Please, please, please tell about the palace and the prince and the earrings," Chelsea begged.

"I'm about to," Gooney Bird said.

Gooney Bird took Napoleon back to his house. The prince asked Gooney Bird to go to the palace for a reward.

"Did you get all dressed up in a ball gown?" Beanie asked.

"Maybe a tiara?" asked Tricia.

"I hadn't planned to describe clothes," Gooney Bird said, "but since you asked, I'll insert a little descriptive passage here."

When she went to the palace, Gooney Bird was wearing clothes from the L.L.

Bean catalogue. She wore Island Hopper shorts with front flap pockets, and a
pointelle knit tank top in Sun Yellow.

The prince had on rugged canvas
shorts and polyester and nylon pale
khaki plaid short-sleeved . . .

Malcolm disappeared under his desk. Ben
picked up his arithmetic book and began to do
some problems. Nicholas put his head down
on his arms and closed his eyes.

Gooney Bird stared at them. "Am I boring
you?" she asked.

"Yes," the class said. All but Felicia Ann,
who was silent, and Keiko, who was not bored
at all.

"What color were the Island Hopper shorts?"
Keiko asked. "I hope blue."

"As a matter of fact, they were Deep Sea
Green, with True Blue stripes down the sides. I
might wear them to school on Wednesday."

"Oh good," Keiko said.

"I'll continue now," Gooney Bird said.

It doesn't matter what clothes the prince had. The main character in this story is Gooney Bird, and it is important to tell a lot about the main character because the main character is right smack in the middle of everything. All the others are just minor characters and it is boring to tell about their clothes.

"Or you could call them *secondary characters*," Mrs. Pidgeon pointed out. "Excuse me for interrupting, Gooney Bird. But I'll just write that on the board: *secondary characters*."

Gooney Bird waited patiently while Mrs. Pidgeon wrote. Then she breathed deeply and was about to continue. But she looked at the class.

She walked down the classroom aisle to Malcolm's desk and peered under it. Malcolm was asleep on the floor.

Ben was doing his arithmetic, and Nicholas

was making his thumbs wrestle with each other. His left one was winning.

"This is my fault," Gooney Bird said loudly. "I have failed to hold your attention. Of course it didn't help that Mrs. Pidgeon interrupted. But I blame myself for not inserting enough suspense into the story.

"Stories need suspense," Gooney Bird said. "So I shall try to add some. Shall I continue the story now?"

"Yes," Mrs. Pidgeon said.

"Yes," said the children, all but Malcolm, who was still asleep, and Felicia Ann, who never said anything.

So Gooney Bird continued. "I'll start right off with a *suddenly*," she said. "That always wakes people up."

Suddenly, when they entered the palace, Gooney Bird needed to go to the bathroom.

Malcolm woke up. He popped up from under his desk. "I have to go to the bathroom," he said.

"Go," Mrs. Pidgeon told him, and pointed to the classroom door. Malcolm hurried from the classroom.

"Did the palace have bathrooms?" Beanie asked. "Oh, I'm sorry," she added. "I forgot to raise my hand."

"Yes," Gooney Bird said. "The palace had two bathrooms. Gentlemen and Ladies."

"And what about the diamond earrings?" Tricia asked.

"I'll finish the story now," Gooney Bird said.

When she came out of the ladies' room, Gooney Bird Greene saw a gumball machine.

"In a *palace?*" Keiko said.

"Shhhh," the other children said.

Gooney Bird continued.

Gooney Bird had not had a gumball for at least four months. She wanted one. And she had brought her money collection, since she always carried it everywhere in a very heavy Ziploc bag. Her arms had developed big muscles from carrying her money collection.

Gooney Bird stopped the story for a moment and held up her arms to display the muscles. Then she went on.

So Gooney Bird took a penny from her money collection and put it into the gumball machine. But instead of a gumball, out came a diamond earring! It was quite a pleasant surprise, and she screwed it onto her left ear.

After that, she felt lopsided. But she

could see that there was another diamond earring inside the gumball machine.

So she put in another penny. She got a blue gumball.

"It probably matched the True Blue stripes in her Sea Green shorts," Keiko pointed out in a loud whisper.

"Shhhh," said the class.

Gooney Bird continued.

Gooney Bird put the blue gumball into her mouth. It made a large lump in her cheek, and it tasted like spearmint.

She felt doubly lopsided now.

So she took another penny from her money collection and put it into the gumball machine. This time she got a yellow gumball. She put the yellow gumball into her mouth, and now she had a large lump on either side of her face, so her face wasn't lopsided, but her head still felt lopsided because she had only one diamond earring.

So she put another penny in, and she got a red gumball. She put it into her pocket to save for later. Now her hips felt lopsided. She took another penny from her money collection.

This time she got an orange gumball and put it into her other pocket, and now her hips weren't lopsided anymore, but she still had only one diamond earring.

Gooney Bird stopped the story and looked at the class. "I am going to jump ahead now," she said. "Mrs. Pidgeon, is there a word for when an author jumps ahead in a story and skips over some things?"

Mrs. Pidgeon thought about it. "When an author jumps *backwards* in a story, it is called a 'flashback.' So maybe jumping ahead would be called a 'flash-forward'?"

"Well," Gooney Bird announced, "I am flashing forward."

After twenty minutes, all of the pennies in Gooney Bird's money collection were gone. And the gumball machine was empty. Now Gooney Bird had sixty-seven gumballs: two in her mouth, two in her pockets, and sixty-three in her Ziploc bag.

Also, she had a pair of very large, glittery, dangly diamond earrings, which she wears to this day.

When they saw her in the diamond earrings, everyone in the palace, including the prince, two motorcycle guys, and a lady in a wheelchair, cheered. Then they hugged and kissed and did a short but quite beautiful ballet.

The End

"What a lovely story!" Mrs. Pidgeon said.

"And the flash-forward was very effective, Gooney Bird. I'm so glad you finally got the second earring."

Gooney Bird turned her head from side to side so her classmates could admire the earrings. All of the children clapped.

"Did the prince ask you to marry him?" Keiko asked.

"What are you talking about?" Gooney Bird said. "The Prinns are already married. Mr. Howard Prinn is married to Mrs. Amanda Prinn. One Prinn plus one Prinn equals *Prinns*. The Prinns lived next door to me with their dog, Napoleon."

"Oh," the children said. *"Prinns."*

Barry Tuckerman had jumped up and was waving his arm frantically in the air.

"That wasn't a true story!" Barry called out.

"I tell only absolutely true stories," Gooney Bird said impatiently. "How many times must I tell you that?"

"No, it wasn't, because I've seen lots of pictures of palaces, and they have throne rooms, and red carpets, and people get dressed up in ball gowns, and —"

"Barry, Barry, Barry," Gooney Bird said with a sigh. "What am I going to do with you?"

"What do you mean?" Barry asked.

"You're talking about a small-p palace. But I was talking about a capital-letter ice cream shop called The Palace, where they have —"

"Bathrooms!" Beanie suggested.

"And a gumball machine!" Chelsea said. "With diamond earrings!"

"Exactly right," Gooney Bird said, and she took her seat. Then carefully she unscrewed her dangling earrings. "Ouch," she said. "These really hurt."

Malcolm returned to the classroom. "Did you get out of jail, Gooney Bird?" he asked.

Gooney Bird looked unhappy for a moment. "No," she said. "Napoleon ate my Monopoly game."

5.

On Tuesday, all of the children, including Felicia Ann, arrived at school early — even Malcolm, who had never been early before.

Tricia had a flower in her hair.

Ben was wearing a vest.

Keiko had a tiny bit of pink lipstick on her lips.

And Barry Tuckerman was wearing a polka dot bow tie.

"Good morning, class," Mrs. Pidgeon said. "Don't you all look nice today!"

"You do, too, Mrs. Pidgeon!" the children said, and Mrs. Pidgeon blushed.

"Well," she said, "I thought I'd wear my new shoes today." Usually Mrs. Pidgeon wore soft, comfortable shoes. But today she was wearing very shiny high-heeled shoes with gold buckles.

The principal, Mr. Leroy, made announcements on the intercom. He announced a bake sale and a birthday and a meeting of the crossing guards.

A fifth grade boy read a poem about Christopher Columbus over the intercom. Everyone in the school said the Pledge of Allegiance together. Then it was time for school to begin.

But Gooney Bird wasn't there.

"Well," Mrs. Pidgeon said, "let's take out our social studies books, class. Let's turn to the chapter called 'Cities.'"

"But Gooney Bird isn't here!" Nicholas called.

"No," Mrs. Pidgeon said, "she isn't. She seems to be absent today. Maybe she has the chicken pox."

The class was silent. The room seemed sad. The lights seemed dim. Even the gerbils, who usually scurried noisily around in their cage, were very subdued. George Washington, in his portrait on the wall, looked as if he might cry any minute.

Slowly the children took their social studies books from their desks and turned to the chapter called "Cities."

Keiko began to cry very quietly. "I don't want to do social studies," she whimpered. "I feel too sad."

Malcolm crawled under his desk and curled up in a ball.

Suddenly the door to the room burst open.

"It's Gooney Bird!" everybody called. The lights seemed to brighten. The gerbils began to run in a circle, and George Washington seemed to smile.

Gooney Bird was out of breath. "I'm sorry I'm late," she said. "I am never, ever late for anything. I always set three alarm clocks, and I

lay out my clothes the night before, and I even put toothpaste on my toothbrush before I go to bed so that I can brush my teeth quickly in the morning! But today —

"Wait," she said. "I have to catch my breath." She stood in front of the class and took a few deep breaths. "There," she said. "I'm fine now."

She smoothed her red hair, which was flying about, and tucked it behind her ears. Today Gooney Bird was wearing gray sweatpants, a sleeveless white blouse with lace on the collar, and amazing black gloves that came up above her elbows.

"This morning," she explained, "I quite unexpectedly had to direct an orchestra."

"An orchestra?" asked Mrs. Pidgeon.

"Yes. A symphony orchestra."

Mrs. Pidgeon smiled. "I hear all sorts of interesting excuses for tardiness, but I have never heard that one before."

"I believe I'm unique," Gooney Bird said.

"Yes, you are, indeed. Did you wear your gloves when you were directing the orchestra?"

"Yes," said Gooney Bird, "as a matter of fact, I did. I found them very helpful."

All of the second-graders had their hands in the air and were pretending to lead orchestras. Even Malcolm was back in his seat, using two pencils as orchestra batons.

Gooney Bird headed toward her desk. She looked around at the other children's open books. "I see we're in the middle of social studies," she said.

Mrs. Pidgeon slipped one foot out of a high-heeled shoe and rubbed it with her hand. Then she put her shoe back on. "Actually," she said, "I think the class would appreciate it if we held story time a little early today."

"YAY!" called all the children, and they closed up their social studies books.

"A Gooney Bird story?" Gooney Bird asked.

"Yes," said Mrs. Pidgeon.

"YES!" called all the children.

Gooney Bird smoothed her long gloves. She went back up to the front of the room. "Which one would you like today?" she asked. "'How Catman Was Consumed by a Cow'?"

"I'd certainly like to hear about Catman and the cow sometime," Mrs. Pidgeon said. "Maybe tomorrow? But this morning I'd like to hear one called 'Why Gooney Bird Was Late for School Because She Had to Direct a Symphony Orchestra.'"

"Oh," Gooney Bird said. "All right. I could tell that."

"And it will be absolutely true?" asked Mrs. Pidgeon.

"Of course," Gooney Bird said. "Have you forgotten? All of my stories are absolutely true."

Then she curtsied, and began.

Why Gooney Bird Was Late for School Because She Was Directing a Symphony Orchestra

Once upon a time, in fact it was just this morning, Gooney Bird Greene got up and got dressed in the clothes that she had carefully laid out the night before.

She ate her breakfast, brushed her teeth with her pre-pasted toothbrush, gathered up her homework, put on her elbow-length gloves, and started off to the Watertower Elementary School.

Gooney Bird interrupted herself. She explained to the teacher and the class, "Sometimes stories start in the most ordinary way. Then they become exciting when something unexpected happens. Don't you find that to be true?"

The children nodded, thinking about their favorite stories.

"Like *Where the Wild Things Are*," Ben suggested.

"Or *Little Red Riding Hood*," Beanie said.

"When the wolf appears, and you don't expect it!"

"Oh, I'm so scared of the wolf!" Keiko whispered loudly. "Every time the wolf appears, I —"

"Shhhh," the children said.

Gooney Bird continued.

> Gooney Bird walked down Park Street, and turned the corner onto Walnut Street, and when she was halfway down Walnut Street, halfway to school, suddenly . . .

She paused. "I've explained before," she said, "about the word *suddenly*. It makes things exciting. Sometimes, class, if you're creating a story and you get stuck, just say the word *suddenly* and you won't have any trouble continuing at all."

"What a good idea!" Mrs. Pidgeon said. "We should start a list called 'Writing Tips.' What happened suddenly on Walnut Street, Gooney Bird?"

Gooney Bird continued.

Suddenly she saw an enormous red and white bus coming, very slowly. Each window had a head in it. The bus was quite full of people.

Gooney Bird was amazed. Even though she had lived in Watertower only a short time, about a week, she knew that the town of Watertower did not have enormous red and white buses.

Watertower had two medium-sized yellow school buses, Gooney Bird knew. And she knew, also, that one of the Watertower churches had a small white bus, really a long van, that had a rainbow painted on it, and said *JESUS IS LORD* on each side.

But an enormous red and white bus was completely new to Watertower.

As Gooney Bird watched, it moved very, very slowly down Walnut Street. She could see that the driver, though he was steering carefully, was also trying to look at a map in his hands.

The bus driver saw Gooney Bird, and he beeped his horn a very small beep. He pulled the bus to a stop with a breathy sound of brakes. Then he pushed the handle that opened the folding door.

"Excuse me?" the bus driver said. "You look as if you're on your way to school."

"Yes, I am," Gooney Bird replied, "and I certainly don't want to be late. I am never, ever late."

The bus driver looked as if he might begin to cry. "I feel exactly the same way," he said. "I am never, ever late. But this morning I have a terrible problem." He held up his unfolded map.

"Do you need help folding your map?"

Gooney Bird asked. "It *is* hard to fold a map. But I find that if you follow the creases very carefully —"

"No," the bus driver said. "My problem is that I'm lost."

"Oh, dear," Gooney Bird said.

"And," the driver continued, "we are going to be late for a concert."

"A concert?"

"Yes. I have an entire symphony orchestra on this bus."

Gooney Bird paused. "Questions about orchestras?" she asked. "Class?"

Barry Tuckerman was waving his hand wildly. "We know all the parts of an orchestra! We listened to *A Young Person's Guide to the Orchestra*!"

"Winds!" Ben called.

"Strings!" Tricia called. She pretended to play an imaginary violin.

"Brass!" Chelsea called. She tried to make a trombone noise, not very successfully.

"Percussion!" said Malcolm loudly, and he began to tap his two pencils in rhythm on his desktop.

"And also," Barry called out, his hand still waving, "we listened to *Peter and the Wolf*!"

"Oh," Keiko said in a small voice, "I hate when the wolf comes. Every time the wolf appears, I —"

"Shhhh," the children said.

Gooney Bird continued.

So Gooney Bird climbed up the steps and got on the bus.

Every seat was filled. There were men and women in the bus, all of them dressed in black. All the men were wearing black turtleneck shirts. The women were all wearing long black skirts.

They definitely looked like an orchestra. But they looked very distressed.

"Where are you supposed to go?" Gooney Bird asked the bus driver.

"To the Town Hall Auditorium," he said. "We are supposed to play a concert there this morning." He looked at his watch. "It begins in twenty minutes," he said in a worried voice.

"I will get you there," Gooney Bird said.

The bus driver called to the orchestra players. "This wonderful girl is going to direct us!" he said.

"Yay!" the orchestra players all called.

Luckily, even though she had lived in Watertower for only a week, Gooney Bird knew exactly where the Town Hall Auditorium was, because her father had pointed it out when they drove around the town.

"There is the hospital," her father had said. "Go there if you happen to see a bank robber on the loose.

"And there is the Town Hall Auditorium," her father had said. "Go there if you want to see a ballet or a concert."

"Start the bus," Gooney Bird told the driver, "and turn right at the very next corner." It was a good thing that she was wearing her long black gloves, When she pointed, everyone could see her long black pointing finger.

There was no place for Gooney Bird to sit down. And we all know that it is dangerous to stand while a bus is going. But she had no choice. She stood beside the driver and held on to the side of his seat. He promised to drive very, very carefully.

"Next, turn left," Gooney Bird said, and pointed.

"And there we are!" she told him. "See that large brick building? That is the Town Hall Auditorium!"

"Yay!" the orchestra players called again. The women began to comb their hair.

"Thank you for directing us!" they all said to Gooney Bird as they got out of the bus. The driver had opened the luggage compartment and was lifting out cellos.

"You will be late to school," one man said as he picked up a large black case. "Trombone," he explained.

"Yes, I will," Gooney Bird said. "I will be tardy."

"Is there some way that we can thank you for leading our orchestra?" he asked.

Gooney Bird thought for a moment. Finally she thought of a way, and she whispered it to the trombone player.

He nodded. "Yes," he said. "We will do that."

One by one the musicians thanked

Gooney Bird. She said goodbye and hurried down the street to Watertower Elementary School.

She arrived at school just as the class was about to read "Cities" in their social studies books.

The End

"Questions, anyone?" Gooney Bird asked.

"Was there a drum player?" Malcolm asked.

"Yes," Gooney Bird said. "Every single part of a symphony orchestra was there. Even a harp."

"Oh," Malcolm said, sighing. "I wish I could have seen the drum player. I love drums."

"You will," Gooney Bird said.

"Was there a flute player?" Chelsea asked.

"Two," Gooney Bird said.

"I wish I could hear the flute players," Chelsea said.

"You will," Gooney Bird said.

"I have a question, Gooney Bird," Mrs. Pidgeon said. "What was it that you whispered to the trombone player?"

"Secret," Gooney Bird said. "But you'll find out at twelve o'clock sharp."

"That's lunchtime," Mrs. Pidgeon pointed out.

"Precisely," Gooney Bird said. "Now, shall we turn to our social studies?"

All morning the children, and Mrs. Pidgeon, too, glanced again and again at the big clock on the wall. They did social studies and arithmetic and had a snack in the middle of the morning. Then they did reading and art. Finally, just as the clock hands moved to twelve o'clock and the second-graders were about to reach for their lunch boxes, Gooney Bird announced, "Here they are!"

She pointed to the large windows on the side of the classroom. The children all stood up and watched through the windows as a red and white bus pulled up and parked.

When the door of the bus opened, the orchestra players came out one by one, holding their instruments. They arranged themselves in a semicircle on the lawn, facing the Watertower Elementary School.

The conductor, holding a baton, stepped to the center and lifted his arms.

"Too bad he doesn't have long black gloves," Gooney Bird murmured.

Mrs. Pidgeon opened the windows so that they could hear better. The orchestra began to play a slow, stately melody.

When it was finished, the conductor bowed. Then he turned to the windows and explained, "That was a sarabande. It's a kind of dance. We'll play it one more time, in honor of Gooney Bird Greene."

So the orchestra played the short sarabande again, and the children danced around the classroom in a very serious and graceful way.

6.

"Today," Gooney Bird said on Wednesday, "I am going to tell you about Catman and the cow. Maybe you've noticed that I'm wearing my cat and cow outfit today."

The students nodded their heads. They *had* noticed. Gooney Bird was wearing an orange fur jacket. Over her shoulder was slung a purse made from brown and white cowhide.

"Sometimes storytellers have special outfits that they wear. I think that's fine as long as it doesn't interfere with the story," Gooney Bird continued. "You can buy fake cat whiskers and ears, for example. But I would never wear such a distracting costume."

"Would you wear a tail?" Beanie asked. "I know somebody who had a cat tail and ears at Halloween."

"Put on your thinking caps, class," Gooney Bird said. "Think back to when I talked about Catman last week."

"No tail!" the entire class said, all except Felicia Ann, although she looked up from the floor.

"That's right. Catman has no tail. I would tell about the lawn mower accident and it would be an absolutely true story, but I never use violence in my stories."

"Oh, good," Keiko said. "Violence makes me cry."

Gooney Bird smoothed her fur jacket and did her breathing exercises. Deep breath. Let it out. Deep breath. Let it out. "I know a lot of you have been worried about Catman," she began.

"I certainly have," Mrs. Pidgeon said. "I've been thinking about Catman ever since he flew out of that flying carpet."

"By the way, Mrs. Pidgeon," Gooney Bird said, "I do want to mention how lovely you look today."

Mrs. Pidgeon blushed a little. She was still wearing her high-heeled shoes with the buckles, and today she was also wearing a rhinestone butterfly perched in her hair.

"In fact, the whole class looks quite lovely," Gooney Bird pointed out. She looked around. "Malcolm, would you stand up?"

Malcolm rose from his seat and held his shoulders back. He was still wearing his polka dot bow tie, and today he had added a plaid belt.

"Keiko?" Gooney Bird said.

Keiko giggled and stood. She had a bright green bow in her hair and a long shiny silk scarf wrapped around her neck.

"Me?" called Chelsea. "Can I stand up?" She

did, and the class could see that she was wearing a fringed cowboy vest over her best dress.

"Me! Me!" Everyone, all but Felicia Ann, was calling out now, but Gooney Bird said, "Later. After the story. I'm ready to begin now."

She took one more deep breath, let it out, and began.

Beloved Catman Is Consumed
by a Cow

Once upon a time, not long ago, after they had left China, Gooney Bird and Catman found themselves flying through the air on a carpet. The carpet landed in a meadow, near a large brown and white cow who was contentedly eating wildflowers. The flowers were purple loosestrife.

The carpet unrolled, and Gooney Bird stood up and looked around. She could see, in the distance, her father's car quickly disappearing down the road.

Beside her, Catman also stood up. He had become very furry and fat, the way cats do when they are frightened.

"My cat becomes very enlarged when my brother brings his dog to visit," Mrs. Pidgeon said. Then she put her hand to her mouth. "Oh! I'm sorry, Gooney Bird. I interrupted."

"That's all right," Gooney Bird replied. "Maybe this is a good time for everyone to tell cat-getting-big-suddenly stories."

Many children did. Barry Tuckerman's grandmother's cat became huge and his tail stood straight out in the air when a groundhog appeared in the yard.

Chelsea's cat became enormously fluffy and hissed and spat when the veterinarian gave her a shot.

Tricia told how her cat got very, very fat and then one day had seven kittens inside the laundry basket.

"Good. So you all understand about cats. Now I'll continue," Gooney Bird announced.

The cow, who had some purple blossoms dangling from her mouth, looked very surprised when a person and a cat and a carpet all landed in her meadow. She thought about what to do and decided that moving to a different corner of the meadow would be the best choice. Carefully, moving slowly in a cowlike fashion, she strolled away toward a corner where yellow cosmos and oxeye daisies were in bloom.

Gooney Bird's attention was on the car, which had now disappeared around a bend in the road. She was a little worried about the disappearance of the car.

But Catman didn't care about the car. Catman had never liked the car at all. In fact, Catman had hated the car, and he was glad that it had disappeared.

But he was very interested in the cow. Catman had never seen a cow before. Now he watched with fascination as the cow moved slowly toward the other corner of the meadow.

He liked the way the cow walked, heavily and with determination.

He liked the way the cow smelled, of thick, sun-warmed cowhide and meadow flowers.

And, as he scampered along behind the cow and the cow noticed and mooed, Catman liked the way the cow *sounded*. It was comforting, the low, throaty sound of a moo, and in the background was the buzzing of flies.

Catman began to purr. In the distance, he could hear Gooney Bird calling "Catman! Catman!" But he didn't care. He found himself falling in love with the cow.

"I like romance," Beanie said.

"Me too," Keiko said with a tiny sigh.

Gooney Bird waited a moment, but no one else said anything. She continued the story.

In the evening, the farmer, Mr. Henry Schinhofen, came to the meadow and called the cow. It was time to take her into the barn to be milked.

The cow liked the farmer, who was soft-spoken and kind; and she liked the barn, which was airy and dark and smelled of hay; and she liked being milked, which felt a little like sneezing: something that needs to be done now and then. So she cheerfully followed the farmer when he called her.

Catman cheerfully followed the cow.

Mrs. Clara Schinhofen, the farmer's wife, was feeding the chickens when her husband walked past, leading the cow. "My word," she said. "Look! There's a

cat with no tail, following the cow!"

"So there is," said her husband. "Perhaps he is hungry. We should feed him."

They tried to take Catman into the house to be fed, but he refused to leave the cow. So they brought him a bowl of tuna fish and gave it to him in the barn. When Mr. Schinhofen milked the cow, he squirted some into a dish for Catman.

That night, Catman, who was by now completely and hopelessly in love, curled up beside the cow and slept. He has slept there ever since. During the day, he goes to the meadow with the cow, and while the cow eats wildflowers, Catman chases field mice and butterflies, listens to the buzzing of flies, and smells the warm and pleasant odor of cowhide.

Gooney Bird paused. "Questions?" she said.

Keiko raised her hand. "I was waiting for the bad part," she said. "I was going to cover my ears."

"What bad part?" asked Gooney Bird.

"You know," Keiko whispered. "Where the cow ate Catman."

Gooney Bird looked surprised. "The cow didn't eat Catman! The cow hardly notices that Catman is there! The cow eats wildflowers."

"But you said —" Keiko began.

"Yes! You said —" Malcolm called.

Mrs. Pidgeon stood up. "Remember the title of the story, children," she said.

They all tried. "'How a Cow Ate Catman,'" Barry Tuckerman called out.

"'How Catman Got Eaten Up by a Cow,'" Tricia said.

Mrs. Pidgeon shook her head. She picked up her notebook. "I wrote it down," she told them. "'Beloved Catman Is Consumed by a Cow.'"

"Let me finish," Gooney Bird suggested. She went on with the end of the story.

That night the farmer and his wife turned on the TV and saw the interview with the little girl who rode a flying carpet.

"If anybody finds my cat," the little girl (it was Gooney Bird) said, "please call the TV station."

So Mr. Henry Schinhofen, the farmer, called.

"I have that cat here in my barn," he said. "Orange and white cat, no tail.

"But I gotta tell you," he said, "I don't think you'll be able to take it away. It won't leave my cow."

"Won't leave your cow?" the TV lady said. She sounded puzzled.

"Nope," said the farmer. "Wouldn't even leave for tuna fish. We had to take the tuna fish and put it right beside the cow."

"Why?"

"Happens sometimes," the farmer explained. "I'd guess you'd call it something like love. That cat is downright consumed by the cow."

"And is the cow consumed by the cat?" the TV lady asked.

"Nope. The cow doesn't care one way or another. But she doesn't step on the cat. She's a careful cow."

The TV people called Gooney Bird and her parents. They told them where Catman was, and that Catman was consumed by a cow.

So the Greene family drove their car back to the meadow and visited Catman. Catman was nice to them, but they could tell that he was not consumed by the Greene family. He was consumed only by the cow.

So they kissed him goodbye. Then they hugged and kissed the farmer and his wife, and they all sang "Farmer in the Dell" and danced in a circle, on their tiptoes. They all lived happily ever after.

The End

"I love happy endings," Keiko said with a sigh.

"Me too," Mrs. Pidgeon said. "Thank you, Gooney Bird. Let's get out our arithmetic books now, class."

Everyone in the class groaned.

"I know," Mrs. Pidgeon said, laughing. "It's much more fun to listen to Gooney Bird's stories. But we can look forward to tomorrow. She'll have another one tomorrow."

Gooney Bird had gone back to her desk and taken out her arithmetic book. She looked up in surprise. "No, actually I won't," she said. "That was my last story."

The second-graders, almost every one of them, called, "No!" in very loud, sad voices.

It sounded like a huge chorus singing a song called "Noooooo!"

Mrs. Pidgeon looked horrified. "But, Gooney Bird!" she said. "We still have a lot of unanswered questions!"

"Like what?" asked Gooney Bird.

"Well, let me think." Mrs. Pidgeon frowned.

"The false teeth!" Nicholas called.

"Yes," Mrs. Pidgeon said. "Why did your father have to pack forty-three sets of false teeth? That's a story you haven't told yet."

Gooney Bird looked surprised. "That's not a story," she said. "That simply requires a dictionary. You have one right there on your desk, Mrs. Pidgeon."

Mrs. Pidgeon reached for her dictionary.

"Look up this word," Gooney Bird said. She pronounced the word very carefully. *"Prosthodontist."*

"My goodness!" Mrs. Pidgeon read the definition. "It's a special kind of dentist. He makes false teeth!"

"Exactly," Gooney Bird said. "That's what my father is. No story there."

"But we want more stories, Gooney Bird!" Barry Tuckerman said in a loud voice. As usual, he was standing up with one knee on his desk chair.

Gooney Bird sighed impatiently. "I need to do my arithmetic," she said. "I'm not very good at subtraction yet. But all right. Sit down, Barry. Close the dictionary, Mrs. Pidgeon. I will tell you how to get stories."

7.

Gooney Bird looked around the classroom. She slid the strap of her cowhide purse from her shoulder and set the purse on the floor below the terrarium table. With her face scrunched into a quiet, thinking expression, she unbuttoned her orange fur jacket and hung it on the back of the chair by her desk. Then she returned to the front of the room and faced the class.

She was wearing a blue plaid skirt, a white blouse, black tights, and brown lace-up shoes. There were bright blue hair ribbons in her neatly brushed red hair. She looked ordinary. She looked dignified. She looked wise.

"Out there, invisible, are a lot of stories not yet told," Gooney Bird told the class.

"Absolutely true ones?" Beanie asked in a small voice.

"Yes. Absolutely true ones."

"What are they?" asked Beanie.

"Do you remember that my first story was called 'How Gooney Bird Got Her Name'?" Gooney Bird asked.

"Yes," Beanie replied.

"Well, another is called 'How Beanie Got Her Name.'"

"Before I was born," Beanie said, laughing, "there was a thing called an ultrasound that showed me curled up inside my mom? And I looked just like a bean! My mom said lima bean, and my daddy said no, jelly bean, and so —"

"That's a fine story beginning," Gooney Bird said. "An absolutely true one. You should tell that one on Friday, Beanie."

"What other invisible stories are out there?" Mrs. Pidgeon asked.

"Do you remember that my second story was about how I came from China on a flying carpet?"

"Oh my, yes," Mrs. Pidgeon said. "I had to look up *China* in the atlas."

"Out there, invisible, and waiting," Gooney Bird said, "is a story called — let me think." She closed her eyes.

"Is that the title? 'Let Me Think'?" Malcolm asked.

"No." Gooney Bird opened her eyes. "The story is called 'How Keiko's Family Came to Watertower.'"

Keiko smiled. "Well, they started out on a ship," she said. "First my grandmother and grandfather got on a big ship in Yokohama and went to Honolulu. They were a little scared because they had never been to America before. Mrs. Pidgeon, you should get the atlas out."

Mrs. Pidgeon smiled. "I will, when you tell your story, Keiko. Maybe next Wednesday?"

"Okay," Keiko said. "And I'll bring some

pictures. And how about if I wear a kimono? That wouldn't be distracting, like whiskers, would it?"

"It would be lovely," Gooney Bird said.

"And I could maybe carry a fan, and a parasol?"

Gooney Bird said gently, "That would be a little like whiskers, Keiko."

"Overdoing it?" Keiko asked.

"Overdoing it," Gooney Bird said.

"What about *me?*" asked Barry. "Do I have a story?"

"Of course you do," Gooney Bird told him. "You have stories called 'How Barry Got His Name' and 'How Barry's Family Came to Watertower' and lots of others."

Barry grinned. "Which one should I tell?" he asked.

"Do you remember that my third story was about my diamond earrings?"

Barry nodded.

"My suggestion is that when it's your turn,

Barry, you should tell an absolutely true story called 'When Barry Spent Every Penny He Had on Something He Wanted Really Badly.'"

The class waited and watched Barry Tuckerman as he squinched his face up, thinking. Then he grinned.

"Okay," he said. "I'll tell it! But it's really, really gross."

"Oh, no!" said Keiko. "I hate gross."

"You can cover your ears for Barry's story," Gooney Bird told her. "Wear earmuffs that day. Green ones would go nicely with your red sweater, I think."

"Who else? What else?" the class called.

"My fourth story was called 'How Gooney Bird Directed an Orchestra.'"

Mrs. Pidgeon suggested, "Maybe we could skip that one, Gooney Bird. I know no one in the class has ever led an orchestra."

"Class?" Gooney Bird asked. "Has anyone here ever been late to school because something quite unusual happened?"

Almost every hand went up.

"Malcolm," Gooney Bird said, "maybe that story could be your assignment. It could be called 'Why Malcolm Was Late to School.'"

"It could be about the time I was asleep under my bed and my mother couldn't find me in the morning," Malcolm said, "or the time that I dropped my toothbrush in the toilet and when I tried to get it back I —"

"Oh, no!" Keiko cried, and covered her ears.

"Don't tell it now and give it away, Malcolm," Gooney Bird said. "You work on your story, and make it very suspenseful by adding a *suddenly* in the middle."

Gooney Bird looked around the classroom. All the second-graders had taken out paper and pencils. They were all writing down ideas for their stories.

"And remember my last story, about Catman?" she reminded them. "Has anyone here ever lost a beloved pet?"

Almost every hand went up again. Even Mrs. Pidgeon's.

"Could that be my story, Gooney Bird?" Mrs. Pidgeon said. "I had a parakeet named Brucie, and somehow the door to his cage was left open, and —"

"Next Tuesday," Gooney Bird said. "'How I Lost Brucie.'"

"'And Found Him Again,'" Mrs. Pidgeon said with a happy smile. "My story has a surprise ending."

"Mine will be 'How I Lost Gretchen Guinea Pig,'" Tricia said. "Mine has a sad ending."

"You know what?" Mrs. Pidgeon said, standing up. "It's lunchtime already. Let's skip arithmetic today, class."

The students put the arithmetic books back in their desks. They reached for lunch boxes instead.

Gooney Bird took out a grapefruit, a cucumber, and some dill pickles. "I'm having a completely vegetarian day today," she explained. "But look at this! Dessert! For the whole class!"

She held up a bulky paper bag.

"What is it?" the children asked.

Gooney Bird grinned. "Sixty-three gum-balls," she said. "And after I give them out, I am going to teach you all a wonderful whirling dance called the tarantella."

Suddenly Felicia Ann looked up from the floor. "Shouldn't we all hug and kiss first?" she said in a surprisingly loud voice.

"Thank you for suggesting that, Felicia Ann," Gooney Bird replied. "Of course we should." And so they did.

The End

Gooney Bird
and the Room Mother

I.

It was early November. Mrs. Pidgeon's second grade students were hard at work on their Pilgrim mural, which had been laid out on the floor. All of the desks had been pushed to one side to make room, and the second-graders were on their hands and knees, working with crayons.

Gooney Bird Greene was right in the middle, as usual.

"I like to be right smack in the middle of everything," Gooney Bird always said.

The children's shoes were lined up in the

coatroom because Mrs. Pidgeon had suggested that it would be wise to take them off. If
they walked on the edge of the mural, their
shoes would leave marks.

"We always take our shoes off at home,"
Keiko had said as she untied her sneakers,
"because my family came from Japan, and
in Japan people never ever wear shoes in the
house."

One by one the children had removed their
shoes. Gooney Bird took the longest because
she was wearing hiking boots that laced halfway up to her knees. When, finally, her boots
were unlaced and removed, everyone could
see that Gooney Bird was wearing one red
sock and one yellow one.

"Gooney Bird's socks don't match!" Malcolm called out, pointing.

"Of course they don't," Gooney Bird said.
"I hardly ever wear matching socks."

"Doesn't your mother roll your socks
neatly into balls when she takes them out of

the dryer? Doesn't she match them up very carefully?" Beanie asked.

Gooney Bird thought about that. She looked down at her own feet and wiggled her toes, one set of toes in a red sock, one in a yellow. "No," she said. "My mother puts all of my clean socks in a basket on the floor of my closet. And every day I choose two. Some days I feel like matching, but most days I don't.

"Most often," she went on, "wearing matching things gives me a feeling of ennui."

"Oh, my," said Mrs. Pidgeon. She went to the board and wrote ENNUI in big letters. "Class? You know what to do."

All of the second-graders took their dictionaries out of their desks.

At the beginning of the school year, the classroom had only one dictionary, which sat on Mrs. Pidgeon's desk, next to her coffee mug.

But Gooney Bird Greene, the new student,

had arrived in October. Gooney Bird had very strong opinions about things. She had brought her own very large dictionary from home. On her first day in the classroom, she announced that she thought that every second-grader should have a very large dictionary.

Mrs. Pidgeon, who was not accustomed to Gooney Bird yet, smiled. "We've always just used this one," she said, picking up the dictionary from her desk. It was slightly dusty. "The school provided it. And it's pretty old. But the school budget doesn't allow for bigger or better dictionaries."

"If someone provided newer, more interesting dictionaries, one for each child, would you use them?" Gooney Bird asked.

Mrs. Pidgeon laughed. "Yes," she said. "Of course I would."

"Give me one week," Gooney Bird said.

Exactly one week later, a very heavy box containing twenty-two very heavy dictionaries was delivered to Mrs. Pidgeon's classroom by a man who had tattoos and big muscles. He brought the box in on a wheeled dolly.

"How on earth did you accomplish this, Gooney Bird?" Mrs. Pidgeon asked as she unpacked the dictionaries and passed one to each student.

"I planned my work," Gooney Bird said, "and then I worked my plan."

"What was your plan?" Barry Tuckerman asked as he examined his thick new dictionary.

"First I put on the right outfit."

Everyone giggled. They had known Gooney Bird Greene for only a short time, but each day she had worn a different outfit, and some of her outfits were amazing.

"What did you wear?" asked Keiko. "Pajamas and cowboy boots?" That was what Gooney Bird had worn on her first day at school.

"Of course not. This was for a business-like visit. I wore my long, black, up-to-the-elbow gloves, my silver wet-look ski pants, a T-shirt with a picture of Albert Einstein on it, and my straw hat with a small artificial flower. I think the flower is a camellia."

"And where did you go, wearing your businesslike outfit?" Mrs. Pidgeon asked. She handed a dictionary to Tricia and reached for another.

"I went to the public library. We only just moved to the town of Watertower, as you know. But my parents have always told me that the public library is one of the first places you must visit in a new town. So I did that . . ."

"Wearing your hat with the camellia?" Mrs. Pidgeon asked.

"Yes, of course. I introduced myself to the head librarian, the assistant librarian, the children's librarian, the reference librarian, and the janitor."

"Just the way you introduced yourself to us on the first day? I remember you said—"

All of the children remembered too. They

said it together. *"My name is Gooney Bird Greene and I want a desk right smack in the middle of the room, because I like to be right smack in the middle of everything."*

"Well, why would I say that to the librarians? I didn't want a desk in the library. I wanted dictionaries."

Mrs. Pidgeon was laughing. "And so you said—"

"I said, 'I'm Gooney Bird Greene and I'm new in town and I would like to know what you do with your old dictionaries, because my second grade class needs twenty-two of them.'"

The children all applauded. "And so they sent us the dictionaries!" Mrs. Pidgeon said in delight.

"Nope."

"Oh. Well, what happened?"

"They said that the old dictionaries were in the basement collecting dust, but they didn't have twenty-two, and also the old dictionaries were obsolete—we can look that word up after we get them all unpacked—and anyway what we needed were nice *new* dictionaries."

"These *do* look brand new," Mrs. Pidgeon said, examining one.

Gooney Bird continued. "Then, suddenly . . ."

The class grinned. They loved it when Gooney Bird said "suddenly." They waited eagerly to hear what came next.

". . . the head librarian went to the phone and called a rich man she knew and said, 'Charles, get down here right away, because there's an enterprising young lady you must meet.'

"So a man named Charles came and shook my hand, and—"

"With your glove on? Or did you take your glove off?" Chelsea wanted to know.

"On. He shook it through my glove. Then we talked and had tea, and suddenly . . ."

Everyone grinned again, and waited.

". . . he ordered twenty-two brand-new dictionaries, and here they are."

When the dictionaries had been distributed to every student, Mrs. Pidgeon moved the empty carton to the coatroom. "Gooney Bird Greene," she said, "you are indefatigable."

The students tried to say the word.

"Indefeat . . ."

"Undeff . . ."

"Indeteff . . ."

Mrs. Pidgeon wrote it at the top of the board, in large printing. "Class," she said, "get out your dictionaries. We will have a lesson in dictionary use."

2.

The word INDEFATIGABLE was still on the board, in the upper-right-hand corner, followed by its definition: *never showing any sign of getting tired.* Now, after the discussion about matching socks, Mrs. Pidgeon carefully wrote ENNUI at the end of the word list, because Gooney Bird had said that wearing matching socks gave her a feeling of ennui. The children knew exactly what to do when a new word appeared. They each got out a dictionary and began to look carefully through the pages.

"I found it!" Tricia called out, with her hand raised.

Mrs. Pidgeon pointed to Tricia and she read the definition aloud carefully. *"A feeling of weariness and dissatisfaction."*

"That's right," Gooney Bird said, nodding her head. "That's exactly how I feel when I wear matching socks. Weary and dissatisfied.

"May I be right smack in the middle of the Muriel, Mrs. Pidgeon?" she asked. "I want to work on Squanto. I want to color his feather."

"It's *mural,* Gooney Bird," Mrs. Pidgeon said. "Not Muriel."

"I know that," Gooney Bird replied. "I just like to call it the Muriel. Because of Muriel Holloway in the office."

Muriel Holloway was the school secretary. She had spiked hair and fancy fingernails. If you threw up in school, first you went to the school nurse, and then Muriel Holloway called your mom to come and get you.

"May I be right smack in the middle and do Squanto?"

Mrs. Pidgeon nodded. Gooney Bird knelt in front of Squanto and began to examine her crayons.

"Everyone choose a place on the, ah, mural," Mrs. Pidgeon said. "We want to get it finished before the pageant. Nicholas, could you work on the forest in the background? Chelsea, how about you? Could you do the turkey?"

Gooney Bird had begun to color one of Squanto's feathers blue. But all of the other children remained standing. They were all looking at their own feet. They looked weary and dissatisfied.

"My feet match," Felicia Ann whispered. "I have a feeling of ennui."

"Mine too," Tyrone said loudly. "My feet are the boringest ones in the whole room. I feel a whole lot of ennui. Can I switch one sock with Nicholas?" He sat on the floor and pulled off one white sock.

"Trade with me!" Barry Tuckerman called. He was grabbing at Ben's left foot.

"Me!" Malcolm called loudly. "Someone switch with me!"

"My goodness, class!" Mrs. Pidgeon said. "Can we keep our voices down, please? Look how carefully Gooney Bird is coloring Squanto. We must all get busy on this mural!"

But the class wasn't listening. The children were examining their own feet and their classmates' feet. They were comparing socks and grabbing and yelling.

"You've lost them, Mrs. Pidgeon," Gooney Bird said with a sigh, "and it was my fault. I apologize. I'll try to make it up to you." She stood up. "*Class!*" she said.

Gooney Bird had a very loud voice when she wanted to use it.

"*CLASS!*" she said again.

The children looked up. They became quiet.

"Here is what we are going to do," Gooney Bird announced. "Arrange yourselves in a circle, please. Try not to step on the Muriel."

She reached out and took the hands of the children nearest to her, Tyrone on one side and Ben on the other. Tyrone reached for Chelsea. Ben took Beanie's hand. One by one the children arranged themselves in a circle around the mural.

Mrs. Pidgeon entered the circle by taking the hands of Nicholas and Chelsea and standing between them.

"Now," Gooney Bird announced, "at the count of three, we will each remove our left sock. One. Two."

"Oh, dear," Mrs. Pidgeon said, "I'm wearing pantyhose. I think I'd better drop out."

Gooney Bird nodded. "You be the supervisor," she suggested.

"Ready?" Gooney Bird said loudly. "*THREE*. Left socks off."

Every child, including Gooney Bird, removed a left sock.

"You'd better help Malcolm, Mrs. Pidgeon," Gooney Bird said. "Remember, he has that problem with left and right?"

Mrs. Pidegon nodded. She went to Malcolm and pointed out his left foot.

"Ready?" Gooney Bird said. "Everyone got that left sock off?"

The children nodded. They wiggled the toes on their bare left feet and waited for their instructions.

"At the count of three, pass your left sock to the person on your left. That will be the person beside your bare foot. Malcolm, Mrs. Pidgeon will help you. One. Two. Ready? *THREE*."

Each child handed a sock to another child.

"I got a *girl* sock," Tyrone said. "I don't want no girl sock."

"A sock is a sock," Gooney Bird said. "Anyway," she added, "you happen to have Chelsea's sock, and Chelsea is one of the smartest girls in this class. Some of her smarts may still be in that sock and they may rub off on you, Tyrone. You've got a very lucky sock there.

"Now. You can all guess what comes next, on the count of three. You put on your new sock. One. Two. *THREE*."

In a moment all the children were wearing unmatched socks. Even Gooney Bird's original pair of one red, one yellow, had become a pair of one red, one white with a blue stripe.

They all looked down and admired their feet.

"There is not a single pair of boring feet in this classroom now," Gooney Bird announced.

"Except mine," Mrs. Pidgeon said with a laugh.

"Except Mrs. Pidgeon's," Gooney Bird agreed. "Now, class, on the count of three . . ."

"Do we switch socks *again?*" Beanie asked.

"Nope. We get to work on this Muriel, because it needs to be done by the pageant. One. Two.

"THREE."

Very shortly after the count of three, when all the children had picked up their crayons and gone to work, the intercom squealed and a deep voice spoke.

"This is your principal, John Leroy. Good morning."

"Good morning," the children said to the intercom.

"We should have done this last month," Mr. Leroy explained, "or even in September. But I got busy with the selection of crossing guards, and I had to deal with certain issues and problems of playground behavior, as you know . . ."

He paused. Malcolm looked up guiltily. Malcolm had been a playground behavior problem.

". . . but now it is definitely time to select room mothers. We will need a room mother for each classroom. Teachers, please ask your students to inquire at home. If . . . ah, just a minute . . ."

Through the intercom they could hear Muriel Holloway whispering to Mr. Leroy. Then he returned to the microphone.

"I have been reminded that last year we did have a room *father* in the third grade. Bailey Stevenson's father did an admirable job, his cupcakes were unusually fine, and we're sorry that he has found a job and is not available again this year. Well, we're not sorry that he found a job. That's not what I meant at all."

Mr. Leroy coughed and cleared his throat. "I meant that we will miss Mr. Stevenson's cupcakes. Now back to work, students. And teachers? By Friday I would like you to turn the names of the room mothers in to Muriel Holloway in the office.

"Have a good day."

The intercom squealed, buzzed, and turned silent. Carefully Gooney Bird began to color Squanto's second feather red, just beside the blue one.

Felicia Ann looked over at the one red, one blue feathers and smiled. "Like my socks," she pointed out in a whisper.

3.

"My mother says absolutely not, no way, no how," Tyrone announced. "Not unless it pays minimum wage."

Mrs. Pidgeon laughed. "Afraid not," she said. "Room mother is a volunteer job. No pay."

She looked around the room. "Did everyone ask? What did your mothers say?"

Chelsea was scowling. "My mother said if I come home wearing Nicholas's stinky dirty sock again, she's going to call Mr. Leroy and complain. And no, she won't be room mother.

She already did the bake sale and she's treasurer of the PTA. Enough is enough."

"My sock was *not* stinky dirty!" Nicholas bellowed.

"No, it wasn't," Mrs. Pidgeon said. "Those were just grass stains on your sock, Nicholas. Anyone else?" She looked around. "Keiko? Maybe your mom?"

Keiko shook her head. "My mother says she is very sorry but she has to work in our store. My father needs her there."

"Yes, of course he does," Mrs. Pidgeon said. "I've been in your family's store, Keiko. Your mother works very hard.

"You all have hard-working moms, I know," she said with a smile.

"Do you have a hard-working mom, Mrs. Pidgeon?" Beanie asked.

Mrs. Pidgeon's smile turned to a sad look. "Not anymore. My mother is very, very old. She lives in a nursing home. I visit her every Sunday afternoon at the Misty Valley Elderly

Care Facility. I always take her a bouquet of flowers. She seems to like that."

She looked around. "Malcolm? Did you ask your mom?"

Malcolm made a face. "My mom has trip—"

"Oh my goodness, of course she does. How could I forget that? Someone who has brand-new triplet babies at home can't possibly do anything else, and we shouldn't even have asked."

"When I asked her, she screamed," Malcolm said.

"How *are* those babies, Malcolm? How are they doing?"

"Bad," Malcolm said. "They have diarrhea."

"My goodness. No wonder she screamed. Anyone else?" asked Mrs. Pidgeon. "Beanie?"

Beanie shook her head. "My mom takes me to swimming lessons on Monday afternoon, and ballet on Tuesday, and horseback riding on Wednesday, and confirmation class on Thursday, and violin on Friday, and she says if I ask her to do one more thing . . ."

"I understand completely. Anyone else? Felicia Ann?"

Felicia Ann looked at the floor and shook her head.

"Barry?"

Barry said no.

"Nicholas?"

Nicholas was scowling. "My socks are *not* stinky dirty," he said loudly. "Chelsea's socks are stinky dirty. Chelsea's *underpants* are stinky dirty."

Chelsea hit Nicholas over the head with her spelling book.

"Enough, enough," Mrs. Pidgeon said with a sigh. She went to Nicholas and rubbed his head. She glared at Chelsea. "Let's turn to our arithmetic. We'll talk about room mothers

tomorrow. All of you ask again at home. Unless . . ." She looked hopefully around the classroom one more time.

"Gooney Bird?" she asked.

Gooney Bird stood up. Today she was wearing a long velvet skirt and a sweatshirt with a picture of the earth on it.

Mrs. Pidgeon peered at the sweatshirt and smiled. "By the way, I like your shirt, Gooney Bird," she said. "Look, children, at what it says under the globe."

"Mother Earth," they all read aloud.

"We were just talking about mothers," Mrs. Pidgeon pointed out.

"Read my back," Gooney Bird said. She turned around.

They all read the back of her sweatshirt. *"Love Your Mother."*

"Well, fine," Mrs. Pidgeon said. "I wish the earth would volunteer to be room mother. Unfortunately the earth doesn't make cupcakes."

"It would make stinky dirty cupcakes," Nicholas said grouchily.

Mrs. Pidgeon glared at Nicholas. "Did you ask your mother, Gooney Bird? Not Mother Earth. Your *real* mother?" she asked.

"Yes, I tried to cajole her."

Mrs. Pidgeon started to laugh. She always laughed when Gooney Bird used a new and interesting word. She turned and wrote CAJOLE on the board. "Dictionaries, class," she said.

Beanie was the first to find *cajole* in the dictionary. "It's hard reading," she said.

"Of course it is," Mrs. Pidgeon agreed. "It's a grownup dictionary. It stretches your reading skills."

"Stretch stretch stretch," murmured Malcolm as he picked up an elastic band. Mrs. Pidgeon gave him a look. He put the elastic band down.

"Give it a try, Beanie," Mrs. Pidgeon said. "You can do it."

Beanie stood and read the definition of

cajole slowly to the class. *"To persuade someone to do something by flattery or gentle argument, especially after a reasonable objection."*

"So your mother had a reasonable objection, Gooney Bird?" Mrs. Pidgeon asked.

"Yes. She is a terrible cook and her cupcakes are always lopsided, and also she has to go to China on Thursday."

"And so you tried to persuade her with flattery?"

"Yes, I told her that she was a wonderful cook and I had heard a rumor that she might be invited to be chef at the White House, and probably it would be good practice for her, being room mother."

"And that didn't work?" Mrs. Pidgeon was laughing.

"No, she said that if I were Pinocchio, my nose would be three feet long."

Gooney Bird scowled. "She meant I was lying, of course, but you all know that I never ever lie."

All of the children nodded. They knew that everything Gooney Bird said was absolutely true.

"I really *had* heard that rumor. I said it to myself and heard myself saying it. So it was absolutely true.

"But she said no, thank you, she did not want to be room mother, especially if she was going to work at the White House, because she wouldn't have time."

Mrs. Pidgeon pointed to the word on the board. CAJOLE.

In small handwriting she wrote its definition next to it.

"Children," she said, "tonight, please try to cajole your mothers.

"We really, really need a room mother," she said with a sigh.

There was a brief knock on the classroom door, and then, without waiting for a reply to the knock, Mr. Leroy appeared. The children gasped. The principal! Usually he was only a voice on the intercom. But here he was, in person, wearing a dark blue suit and his UNICEF necktie, standing right in front of the second grade.

"Just checking in," he said cheerfully. "I was wondering if —"

Mrs. Pidgeon shook her head. "Afraid not," she said. "Not yet."

"Hmm." Mr. Leroy looked concerned. "Well," he said, "keep me posted."

He turned to leave, then stopped and said, "I like your shirt, Gooney Bird Greene."

"Thank you. Read my back." Gooney Bird turned around.

He read it and smiled. "A very fine admonition," he said. "Love your mother. Yes, indeed." Then he left the room.

"Class," said Mrs. Pidgeon, who was already writing ADMONITION on the board, "get out your dictionaries."

4.

Not a single mom wanted to be room mother.
Not one.

"Oh, dear," Mrs. Pidgeon said with a sigh.
She looked at the board, where the word
CAJOLE was carefully printed near the end
of the word list, just above ADMONITION.
"I guess cajoling doesn't always work."

"Well," said Tricia from her desk, "we
learned a new word, anyway. That's always a
good thing."

Mrs. Pidgeon nodded. "True," she said.
"And you know, class, they say that if you

use a new word three times, it is yours forever."

"Who says that?" asked Beanie.

"I don't know," Mrs. Pidgeon replied.
"They."

Barry Tuckerman stood, suddenly, beside
his desk. *"Cajole, cajole, cajole,"* he said loudly.
"Now it is mine forever. No one else is allowed to say it."

"That isn't exactly what I meant, Barry.
You do not *own* the word. We may all use it.
And in fact, class, I wish you would all try a
little more cajoling at home. This is the only
class in Watertower Elementary School that
does not have a room mother yet. Mr. Leroy
is becoming a little impatient about it.

"Now, though, I think we ought to start
our preparations for the Thanksgiving pageant. The Muriel—I mean the mural—is
coming along well. But we have a song to
learn, and costumes to make, and I have to
select the cast."

"I already have a cast!" Ben called out, holding up his arm. Ben had fallen from his bike a month earlier and broken his wrist. All of the children, and Mrs. Pidgeon, and even the principal, Mr. Leroy, had signed their names on the cast, using different colored markers. The names were faded now, and the cast itself, which had once been white, was gray and dirty, with bits of string like dental floss dangling from it.

Keiko wrinkled her nose and said, "Your cast smells bad, Ben."

"I know," Ben said, making a face. "But next week the doctor takes it off."

"Your arm will be all skinny and wrinkled inside it when they take it off," Barry Tuckerman told him. "My cousin had a cast on his arm and his arm *died* inside the cast."

"Is that true, Mrs. Pidgeon?" Ben asked nervously.

"Your arm is probably dead already. Probably green," Barry added.

Ben's face began to pucker up. "My arm is *dead? Green?*" he wailed.

"Children, children," Mrs. Pidgeon said. "No, Ben, your arm will be fine. Besides, I'm talking about a different kind of cast. We need a cast of characters for the pageant. We need Pilgrims and Native Americans. We also need a turkey, and, let me see, some succotash, and a pumpkin pie. But the food items don't have to be human beings."

"I want to be Squanto!" Gooney Bird said. "I love Squanto. He was always absolutely right smack in the middle of everything."

"Squanto's a *boy!*" Barry called loudly. "Only a boy can be Squanto! Right, Mrs. Pidgeon?"

"Actually," Mrs. Pidgeon said, "I've already made a list. So put your hands down, everyone."

She read the list aloud. There were twenty-two children in the classroom, and each was on the list. Eleven Pilgrims. Eleven Native Americans.

"But who is Squanto?" the children asked.

Mrs. Pidgeon looked around the class. Now every child, not just Gooney Bird and Barry, was waving an arm in the air, volunteering eagerly to be Squanto.

"I haven't decided that yet," Mrs. Pidgeon said. "But I have an idea."

She went to the board, to the list of words.

REWARD, she wrote. "You all know what a reward is," Mrs. Pidgeon said.

"Money!" shouted Ben. "A thousand dollars if you catch a criminal!"

"Well," Mrs. Pidgeon said, "it could be that. But a reward doesn't have to be about criminals. Let's look it up."

Everyone opened the dictionaries and turned the pages. Chelsea raised her hand first. *"That which is given in appreciation,"* she read aloud to the class.

"You see, it doesn't have to be money," Mrs. Pidgeon explained. "And in this case, the reward I am going to give is the important role of Squanto in the pageant. Someone is going to get that role in appreciation. It will be that person's reward."

"Reward for what?" several children asked at the same time. "For catching a criminal?"

"No," Mrs Pidgeon said. She sighed. "For finding me a room mother."

An hour later, after lunch, the second-graders were learning one of the songs for the Thanksgiving pageant. It was a complicated song that Mrs. Pidgeon herself had written. The Pilgrims sang half and the Native Americans sang half. The song was about food.

"Succotash, succotash, lima beans and corn . . ." Mrs. Pidgeon played the notes on the piano and sang the words. "To the tune of 'Jingle Bells,'" she explained. "Ready, Native Americans? This is your part. Try it with me."

Eleven children, including Gooney Bird Greene, sang the succotash lines.

"Now, Pilgrims? Listen to your part. Just like the next two lines of 'Jingle Bells.'" Mrs. Pidgeon played and sang, *"Thank you for the vegetables, On this Thanksgiving morn."*

The Pilgrims sang loudly.

"Now the next verse is about the turkey. Native Americans? Ready to listen carefully?"

Gooney Bird Greene raised her hand. "Does Squanto sing with the Native Americans?" she asked.

"No, actually, while the Pilgrims and Native Americans are singing, Squanto will be carrying the food across the stage. Perhaps Squanto will do some sort of dance. I haven't worked out the details yet."

Beanie, standing with the Pilgrims, raised her hand. "I take ballet lessons!" she said. "Maybe I could be—"

But Mrs. Pidgeon shook her head. "Not ballet, Beanie," she said. "They didn't have ballet in Plymouth. All right, class, let's pay careful attention to the next part. Still the tune of 'Jingle Bells,' remember. *Gobble gobble, here it comes, turkey roasted brown . . .*" She played the melody on the piano while she sang the words. Then the eleven Native Americans sang it after her.

"Mrs. Pidgeon, may I please be excused?" Gooney Bird asked politely. "I need to be excused."

Mrs. Pidgeon paused with her hands on the piano keys. "Is this a seriously urgent need?" she asked.

"Yes."

"All right, then. Be quick."

Gooney Bird slipped out of the classroom while Mrs. Pidgeon sang on. *"Thank you, noble Squanto, you may set the platter dooooowwnn . . ."*

The children were still singing and passing imaginary helpings of food around when Gooney Bird returned a few minutes later.

"Announcement!" Gooney Bird said in a loud voice. "Important announcement!"

Mrs. Pidgeon stopped playing the piano. The room became quiet. All of the children knew that when Gooney Bird had an announcement to make, it was worth listening to.

"I am Squanto," Gooney Bird announced.

"But—" Mrs. Pidgeon began.

"I got us a room mother," Gooney Bird said proudly.

Mrs. Pidgeon clapped her hands. "But how?" she asked.

"Simple phone call. They let me use the telephone in the office. I told Muriel Holloway it was an emergency."

Mrs. Pidgeon frowned slightly. "Well," she said, "it was beginning to feel like an emergency, actually."

"So now I'm Squanto, right?"

"Wait, Gooney Bird! You haven't told us *who* our room mother is!"

"I'll write it down," Gooney Bird Greene said. She went to the board and picked up the chalk. "Class," she said, "get out your diction-aries." She wrote a word very carefully on the board, at the end of the list.

The word she wrote was INCOGNITO.

"This is our room mother's name," she said.

5.

"With the identity disguised or hidden," Mrs. Pidgeon read to the class, from the dictionary. "So our room mother doesn't want us to know who she is?

"Or *he?*" she added, remembering Bailey Stevenson's father.

"It's a she," Gooney Bird said. "I think it's okay to tell you that. But you're right: she wants to be a secret."

"How did you cajole her?" Tricia asked. "Is it *my* mom? I couldn't cajole her. How did you?"

"Is it *mine?*" Barry asked. "I bet it's mine."

"Did you pay her?" Tyrone asked. "If you paid her, it's *mine.*"

"My lips are sealed," Gooney Bird said.

"Maybe it's mine," Keiko said.

"Maybe *mine,*" whispered Felicia Ann. "Oh, I hope mine."

Malcolm was rolling a piece of paper into a tube that looked like a telescope. Malcolm had a very hard time keeping his hands still. He called out loudly, "If it's my mom, and if she brings those three babies to this school, I'm . . . I'm . . ." He scowled and sputtered and wrinkled his face and couldn't decide just what he would do.

"Sealed," Gooney Bird repeated.

"What are your babies' names?" Felicia Ann asked Malcolm. "I love babies."

"I'm not saying," Malcolm replied with a scowl. "My lips are sealed."

Mrs. Pidgeon began to laugh. "Well, class, Malcolm is not going to reveal the triplets' names. And Gooney Bird is not going to reveal the identity of our room mother, though I somehow suspect that it might be someone who has decided that she doesn't want to be chef at the White House . . ."

She looked at Gooney Bird, who shook her head. "Tightly sealed," she said.

"Well, I am delighted that we have one," Mrs. Pidgeon said, "and I will notify Mr. Leroy. But Gooney Bird, would you tell us — without revealing the name, of course — the absolutely true story of how you cajoled her?"

Gooney Bird nodded. "I guess I could do that," she said. She was already standing in the center of the room, and she began to take deep breaths, as she always did when beginning a story.

The Pilgrims and Native Americans all sat down on the floor. Keiko clapped her hands in delight. Malcolm stopped rolling the piece of paper into a tube. Barry crept over to his desk and sat down quietly. Mrs. Pidgeon turned around on the piano bench to listen.

"'How Gooney Bird Got a Room Mother' is the title," Gooney Bird began.

"Sometimes," she explained, "a title should be a little mysterious. It should make you wonder what the story is about. I could have called this one 'An Exciting Phone Call' or maybe . . ."

"'Incognito'!" called Barry from his desk. "That would have been a good title!"

Gooney Bird nodded. "Yes, it would. Good for you, Barry. I might change my title later, actually. You can do that. The title you use first is called the *working* title. And my working title is 'How Gooney Bird Got a Room Mother.'"

She looked down at herself. "You know how usually, in stories, I try to describe what the main character looks like, and what she is wearing?"

The children nodded. They had heard Gooney Bird tell many stories before.

"Well," she said, "in this story, the main character is me, and as you can see, today I am wearing tap shoes, blue tights, red Bermuda shorts, and an embroidered peasant blouse from Bavaria."

"Bavaria!" murmured Felicia Ann. "I never heard of Bavaria before!"

"It's quite an interesting outfit, I think," Gooney Bird said. "But I've decided that it will not be included in the story. This story is going to be an all-dialogue story. No description."

"Class?" Mrs. Pidgeon said. She went to the board and wrote the word DIALOGUE. For a few moments the room was silent except for the pages of the dictionaries turning.

"I found it!" called Ben. He read aloud, *"Words used by characters in a book."*

"Or a story," Gooney Bird said. "Okay. I'm going to begin. There are only two characters in this story. One is Gooney Bird, and the other is . . ."

"Oh, don't tell! She doesn't want you to tell!" several children called.

". . . Mrs. X," Gooney Bird said. "I'm calling her Mrs. X. And I'm starting my story with a sound effect. Listen."

RINNNNG. RINNNNG.

"Hello?" Mrs. X said, when she answered the telephone.

"Hello," said Gooney Bird Greene. "I am calling from Watertower Elementary School."

"Yes? My goodness, is something wrong at the school?" asked Mrs. X.

"I think it was my mom," Keiko said. "She always worries. She worries about chicken pox, and unsanitary restrooms, and earthquakes."

"My mom worries too," said Tricia. "Mine worries about kidnappers and unfriendly dogs."

"Mine worries about undercooked hamburger," said Ben.

"Mine too. And swimming too soon after lunch. And wasps," said Chelsea.

"Not mine," Malcolm said glumly. "My mom only worries about those triplets. And diaper rash."

"Please tell their names, Malcolm. I love babies," Felicia Ann said in her soft voice.

"No. They're incognito."

"Class!" Gooney Bird said impatiently. "You are interrupting the story! Dialogue is supposed to flow along smoothly!"

"Sorry," everyone replied.

"But you did remind me of something: how much all moms worry about their children. So I'm going to interrupt the dialogue and insert something about that."

"What's that called, when you do that?" asked Beanie.

Gooney Bird thought, and then shrugged.

"I don't know," she said. She looked at the teacher. "Mrs. Pidgeon?"

Mrs. Pidgeon thought. Then she said, "That would be called an *authorial intrusion*, I think. When the author intrudes to say something that really isn't part of the story. But I'm not even going to write that on the board. It isn't important."

"Well, here I go, starting up again!" Gooney Bird said. She took a deep breath and continued.

All mothers worry about their children. Not only human mothers, but animals. Once I had a cat who was always looking for her kittens and got very upset if they strayed too far away. Now picture if that cat was a *human* and her children went to school every day and she didn't know what was going on at school, and suddenly someone called and said . . .

Gooney Bird stopped and looked around. Malcolm had started rolling his paper again, and Felicia Ann, seated on the floor, had put her head down on her knees. Chelsea yawned.

"Sorry," Gooney Bird said. "That is why authors shouldn't intrude. It's boring. Back to the dialogue."

"No, Mrs. X," said Gooney Bird. "There is nothing to worry about. I am calling with a request."

"And what might that be? Not a solicitation for money, I hope!" Mrs. X's voice sounded suspicious.

"I bet it's my mom!" said Beanie. "She hates when the phone rings and it's some-one—"

Gooney Bird glared at Beanie.

"Sorry," Beanie said.

"No, I'm calling to tell you that you have been selected for a great honor."

"*Right!* The last time I got a call like that, they told me I had won a trip to Las Vegas," Mrs. X said, "but then it turned out that I was supposed to pay taxes and handling charges and buy a membership in something, I think a health club . . ."

"It's my mother," Barry announced loudly. "I'm sure it's my mother."

"No, it's mine," said Tyrone. "She almost bought a time-share in Mexico and it was a big scam."

"It's *my* mother," Nicholas and Tricia said together.

Gooney Bird glared at all of them. When the room fell silent, she continued.

Gooney Bird explained very patiently. "No," she said, "this is truly a great honor, not a scam at all. You have been chosen as room mother for Mrs. Pidgeon's second grade class."

Mrs. X was silent for a moment. She was dumbfounded. She was overcome.

"Are you still there?" Gooney Bird asked.

"Yes," said Mrs. X.

"So may I tell everyone you said that?"

"Said what?" asked Mrs. X.

"'Yes.' You said, 'Yes.'"

"I only meant, 'Yes, I am still here.'"

"Please, please say yes," Gooney Bird said, "because then I get to be Squanto."

Mrs. X still didn't speak.

"And the principal will stop bugging Mrs. Pidgeon," Gooney Bird added.

"The principal is doing that?" asked Mrs. X in an outraged voice.

"Indeed he is," Gooney Bird replied.

Mrs. X didn't speak.

"The only thing you have to do is provide cupcakes. And you can come to the Thanksgiving pageant if you want, and sit in a seat of honor, and also—"

Gooney Bird looked at Mrs. Pidgeon. "I hope you don't mind, I said the next thing without asking your permission."

"What was that?" Mrs. Pidgeon asked. "I hope you didn't say she'd be paid. You know we don't pay anything."

"I'll continue," Gooney Bird said.

"And also, Mrs. Pidgeon, who wrote quite a fine song about succotash, will compose a second song, and its title will be 'Room Mother.'"

Mrs. Pidgeon began to laugh. "All right," she said. "I can do that."

Gooney Bird looked relieved. She continued.

"And," Gooney Bird told Mrs. X, "we will

all sing the song to you at the end of the Thanksgiving pageant."

There was silence on the other end of the telephone. Then—

Gooney Bird looked at the class. "Guess the next word," she said.

"SUDDENLY!" they all shouted out. They'd learned from Gooney Bird how important the word *suddenly* could be.

"You got it." Gooney Bird continued.

Suddenly Mrs. X started to laugh. And she said, "Yes. I'll do it."

"Thank you, thank you!" Gooney Bird told her.

"On one condition," Mrs. X added.

"What is that?"

"Until Thanksgiving, I am incognito."

"My lips are sealed," said Gooney Bird.

The End

The class clapped. Gooney Bird bowed. Mrs. Pidgeon smiled.

"Gooney Bird," she said, "you are Squanto, for sure."

6.

"Why do we have to have cardboard costumes?" Beanie complained. "At ballet class, we have stretchy satin, and for the recital I have shimmery wings attached. They're gold."

"Hold still," Mrs. Pidgeon told her. "I have to cut this very carefully. I don't want to miss and cut your hair."

Beanie stood very, very still. She looked nervous. "Don't you dare," she said. "I'm growing my hair to my waist."

"Ha!" shouted Malcolm. "Beanie's hair goes to the waste! To the *wastebasket!*"

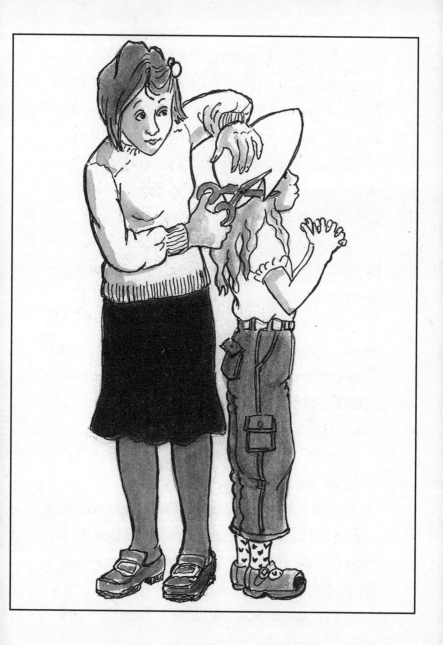

"There," Mrs. Pidgeon said. "You can move now, Bean." She lifted the white cardboard that she had been cutting. "The reason we have cardboard costumes is because we already have cardboard, so it doesn't cost anything. And it makes good Pilgrim hats and Native American headbands.

"Malcolm." She glared at him. "Stop tormenting Beanie. Is your belt buckle almost finished?"

Malcolm nodded and went back to his work. All of the Pilgrim boys were making large cardboard belt buckles. "I saw a guy with a skull on his belt buckle," he announced. "He was a Hell's Angel."

"Cool!" said Ben. "A real skull?"

"No. Fake."

Keiko looked up from the beads she was gluing onto her Native American headband. "Don't talk about skulls," she said nervously. "It makes me feel sick."

"My mom has skull earrings," Tyrone

announced. "She wore them on Halloween. They dangled. Two little skulls."

Keiko stopped gluing beads and put her hands over her ears.

"These belt buckles will be very plain," Mrs. Pidgeon said. "The Pilgrims didn't decorate their clothing. The Native Americans did, though. Look what a good job Keiko is doing." Gently she reached down and removed Keiko's hands from her ears so that Keiko could continue attaching beads before her glue dried.

"Me too! Look at mine!" Tricia held up her headband.

"And mine! Mine's the best!" Nicholas called.

Mrs. Pidgeon walked around the room admiring the work of each second-grader. "I'm proud of all of you," she said, smiling. "Pilgrim girls, even though you don't have decorations, your white bonnets are quite lovely. Chelsea," she said, adjusting Chelsea's cardboard hat, "I think you might want to trim yours back a bit so that it doesn't cover your eyes that way.

"And Native Americans? When you finish your beading, you may each add one feather from the feather pile." She reached for Tyrone's hand, which had quickly grabbed the entire collection of feathers. "Just one, Tyrone. Remember we talked about sharing just yesterday?"

Scowling, Tyrone selected a long yellow feather and put the rest back.

"I wish I could be a Native American," Chelsea said, frowning. "I hate my Pilgrim hat. It's too plain."

Beanie, wearing her white cardboard bonnet, patted Chelsea's arm. "But we were very brave," she reminded her. "We crossed the ocean, remember? And not in a cruise ship, either."

Ben, looking up from under the brim of his tall black Pilgrim hat, added, "Feathers are for babies. Pilgrims were tough and mean. They battled pirates."

"Actually," Mrs. Pidgeon said, "I don't think the Pilgrims encountered pirates at sea. But they certainly were brave. You're right about that, Ben. Can you lift your hat up a little, so your eyes show?"

Ben tilted his head back so that he could see. All of the Pilgrims had their heads tilted back. Somehow the Pilgrim hats were all a little too large.

"Good work, everyone!" Mrs. Pidgeon continued, looking around at the class. "And you've all memorized the words to the food song?"

All of the Native Americans and Pilgrims nodded.

"We'll practice it again when we get the headgear all done."

"Have you written the room mother song, Mrs. Pidgeon?" Gooney Bird asked. She was coloring Squanto's headband carefully.

"I'm working on it. There's a little problem with rhyming," Mrs. Pidgeon said. "If only she'd let us use her *name*—"

"Absolutely not," Gooney Bird said. "Incognito."

"Well, if you'd explain to her what a problem it creates. For example," Mrs. Pidgeon said, "if the song went, *Hail to thee, Room Mother Greene,* then the next line could easily be *Best room mother we've ever seen*—"

Gooney Bird Greene stopped coloring. She glared at Mrs. Pidgeon.

"I just used that as an example," Mrs. Pidgeon explained hastily. "I didn't intend to give anything away. I could have used a different example. *Room Mother Brown,* for instance. *Best room mother in town*—"

Gooney Bird put her hands on her hips. "I talked to her last night, and she said that if anyone says her name, if anyone reveals her identity, she will *not* bring cupcakes and she will not even come to the pageant, no matter how many songs you write."

"Well then, she will remain incognito." Mrs. Pidgeon laughed. "And I'll create the best song I can, under the circumstances."

"Thank you."

"And what about Squanto's dance, Gooney Bird? Have you been working on it?"

Gooney Bird frowned. "Yes. It's hard, though. I keep wanting to do the hula."

"The *hula?*"

"My grandma can do the hula," Keiko said. "She lives in Hawaii."

"That's lovely, Keiko. If she comes to visit, maybe she can give us lessons," Mrs. Pidgeon said.

"*My* grandma can do the funky chicken!" Chelsea said. She stood, with her white Pilgrim hat falling forward, in order to demonstrate.

"Gross!" Nicholas and Ben said together, watching Chelsea wiggle her behind.

Mrs. Pidgeon played a loud chord on the piano in order to get the class's attention. Then she began to play some low notes in a repetitive way. "Pretend this is a drumbeat, Gooney Bird. Squanto should simply move across the stage, keeping time to the sound of drums. Maybe some rhythmic foot-hopping too?"

"I guess so," Gooney Bird said. "I'll work on it at home. And it'll be easier when I have my costume on. I'll feel more like a real Squanto in my costume. I'll feel authentic, then."

Mrs. Pidgeon picked up the chalk and added AUTHENTIC to the word list.

"True and original, known to be trustworthy," Beanie read from her dictionary.

"That's Squanto, all right," said Gooney Bird.

7.

"I've got the room mother song finished," Mrs. Pidgeon announced. She sat down at the piano. "We'll need to learn it quickly because, as you know, the Thanksgiving pageant is next week.

"Gather round," she said. "And now that we've finished the hats and headbands, why don't we wear them while we sing? This will be sort of a dress rehearsal.

"Pilgrims over here." She pointed to the left. "And Native Americans here." She pointed to the right. The second-graders, wearing their headgear, arranged themselves around the piano.

"I can't see!" Nicholas called. His Pilgrim hat had slid down over his eyes. Beanie, her own white bonnet falling across her forehead, leaned over and lifted his hat up. "Stand very still," she told him, "so it doesn't fall down again."

"How about me?" Gooney Bird asked. "Where should Squanto stand? Probably in the middle, right? Because he's the star, right smack in the middle of everything?"

"In the middle is fine," Mrs. Pidgeon said. "What is that on your head, Gooney Bird?"

"Squanto's hat."

"I thought you were making a headband. I *saw* you making a headband."

"I decided Squanto should have a better hat than the other Native Americans, because he's been to England, remember?"

"Well, yes, he did travel there. But that's a

top hat, Gooney Bird. Something an ambassador might wear. I don't think—"

"I think Squanto brought it back from England. He probably went shopping and bought a lot of new clothes there. People always buy new clothes when they travel."

"That's true. My mom went to Hawaii to visit my grandma, and she bought a muu-muu," Keiko said.

"My dad went to Albuquerque on business and he brought back a silver and turquoise belt buckle," Tricia said.

"My mom and dad went . . ." Chelsea began.

Mrs. Pidgeon sighed. She played a chord on the piano, to quiet the children. Then she played a simple melody.

She played it again, and sang, *"Roooommmm Motherrrr—"*

She looked around. "Recognize that? It's the melody from 'Moon River.'"

All of the second-graders shook their

heads. "I know a song about the man in the moon," Beanie said.

"I know one about the cow that jumped over the moon," Ben said.

"I know one about shine on harvest moon," Nicholas said.

"I know a moon song," Tyrone announced. "Listen! *Oh Mister Moon, Moon, bright and shiny moon, please shine down on meeeee!*"

"No, no." Mrs. Pidgeon played the melody again. *"Roooommmm Motherrrr,"* she sang. "Try it with me."

"Roooommmm Motherrrr," all of the children sang. Keiko's headband fell forward across her eyes. She pushed it back up but her bangs got caught.

"I can't see," Felicia Ann whispered. Her Pilgrim bonnet had lurched down over her forehead.

"Oh dear," Mrs. Pidgeon said, turning around on the piano bench. "We're having hat problems of all sorts. Let's not worry about that now, though. We need to learn this song. The next line is . . ." She hesitated. "Well, if we were singing the original song, it would be *wider than a mile* — but of course we don't want the room mother to think we are commenting on how *wide* she is, do we?" Mrs. Pidgeon winked at Gooney Bird.

Gooney Bird shrugged. "I don't think she'd mind," she said.

"I've changed it," Mrs. Pidgeon said. "So we'll sing *kinder than a smile* instead. Give it a try after me, class."

The Pilgrims and Native Americans all sang loudly. *"Kinder than a smile —"*

"Good! Barry? Can you push your headband up?"

Barry tried.

"Ben? Pilgrim hat? Up?"

Ben tried. He wrinkled his face in order to hold his hat brim up.

"Next line: *Your clothing is in style —*"

"Why would we say that, Mrs. Pidgeon?" Gooney Bird asked.

"Well, because it rhymes with *smile*. And although of course I don't *know* our room mother, although she's incognito, I suspect she is quite stylish, right? Because she comes from a stylish family?"

Mrs. Pidgeon looked meaningfully at Gooney Bird, who today was wearing a long flowered gypsy skirt, a leather vest, hiking boots with red laces, and, of course, the top hat that she had explained Squanto would have brought back from his stay in England.

Gooney Bird sighed. "Okay," she said. "Whatever."

"*Hooray*—" Mrs. Pidgeon sang next. "In the original song," she explained, "it says *someday* at that point. But *someday* doesn't work for us, really."

"No," said Malcolm loudly, "because we'll want those cupcakes *right away* after the pageant!"

"Let's try that first verse again from the beginning. Nicholas? Can you see, with your Pilgrim hat down like that?"

"No," said Nicholas from under his hat brim. "But it's okay. I can sing."

"Roooommmm Motherrrr," the second-graders sang enthusiastically, in unison.

Wearing her top hat jauntily and singing as loudly as possible, Gooney Bird began testing some dance steps in the center of the room. "I think Squanto probably learned the tango in England," she explained.

8.

On Tuesday morning of Thanksgiving week, the day before the pageant, Mrs. Pidgeon wrote another new word on the board, below AUTHENTIC. She wrote FIASCO. She sighed, and stared at the word.

"Dictionaries, class," she instructed, though she hadn't needed to. The second-graders had already reached for their dictionaries and begun turning to the *F* section.

Barry Tuckerman waved his hand in the air. "I found it!" he called out. When Mrs.

Pidgeon nodded to Barry, he stood and read aloud, *"A total failure."*

Mrs. Pidgeon sighed. "Correct, Barry. Good dictionary work. The word *fiasco* means a total failure, especially a humiliating one. Say it after me, class."

"Fiasco. Fiasco. Fiasco," the second-graders said aloud.

The gerbils, usually quiet in their cage in the corner, unexpectedly began to fight. They chittered noisily and chased each other in a circle. A paper thumbtacked to the bulletin board suddenly came loose and fluttered to the floor. The radiator hissed. Outside, it was raining in a steady drizzle.

"What's wrong, Mrs. Pidgeon?" asked Beanie. "You look sad. Did we do something wrong?"

"No, no. You children have all worked so hard. I'm very proud of you," Mrs. Pidgeon said. "But I'm worried about the Thanksgiving pageant," she confessed. "I'm afraid it will be a fiasco."

"No, it won't! Look! I got my cast off!" Ben reminded her, holding up his arm. "And my arm works!"

"We sent the invitations," said Felicia Ann. "And, remember, we put turkey stamps on them?"

"The Muriel's done," Barry pointed out. "It turned out great! We only have to hang it up in the multipurpose room."

"The room mother says the cupcakes are all ready for tomorrow afternoon," Gooney Bird said. "And lemonade."

"Yes, you've all done wonderfully. And all of your mothers are coming? I know yours is, of course, Gooney Bird," Mrs. Pidgeon said. "Everyone else? And some dads? And little brothers and sisters?"

All of the children nodded. "And my auntie," Keiko said.

"And my triplets," Malcolm said, making a face. "I hoped they would get chicken pox, but they didn't."

"Please, *please* tell me their names," Felicia Ann begged.

"No," Malcolm said with a scowl. "They don't *have* names."

"Malcolm, Malcolm," Mrs. Pidgeon said, putting her arm gently across his shoulders. "They probably have beautiful names and I hope someday you will tell them to us.

"You children have all worked very hard. It's just that—" She hesitated.

"What?" asked Beanie. "We know all the words to the songs."

"Well, I'm concerned about the songs," Mrs. Pidgeon said. "I'm not really a songwriter, and they seem, well, a little slapdash to me."

She wrote the word on the board.

"Oh, dear," said Ben when he found it in the dictionary. "That's bad."

"I know," Mrs. Pidgeon said, and she wrote

the definition on the board: *"Careless, hasty, unskillful."*

"Our costumes are all made," Tricia added.

"I'm very concerned about the costumes," Mrs. Pidgeon said. "I'm not really a costume designer, and they seem —"

"Slapdash?" asked Tyrone.

"Maybe a little," Mrs. Pidgeon said, "and ill-fitting."

"We know our lines," Nicholas said. "Mine is 'Thank you, good friend Squanto!' I know it by heart."

"I'm concerned about the lines," Mrs. Pidgeon said.

"But you wrote the lines, Mrs. Pidgeon!" Tricia pointed out.

"I know. And I'm not really a writer. The lines are slapdash."

All of the children looked at Mrs. Pidgeon. She looked very sad. Felicia Ann, the most bashful person in the class, went to her and gave her a hug. "You're a very good teacher,

Mrs. Pidgeon," she said. "You don't have to be a writer, or a songwriter, or a costume designer, or even a Muriel maker. Because you're a *teacher*. You taught me to *read!*"

"Me too!" called Tyrone. "I couldn't read worth *nuthin'* when I came to this class! Now lookit! I can read a whole dictionary!"

"Me too!" called Ben. "I only could read baby books before, but now I can read whole long words!"

"We all can!" the other children shouted.

Mrs. Pidgeon began to cheer up. She smiled at the children. "Thank you," she said. "I'm sorry that I was depressed for a minute. It's just that the story of the first Thanksgiving is such a truly wonderful story, about becoming friends, and helping one another, and being thankful. I wish I could have presented it better, instead of writing a dumb song about succotash."

"Mrs. Pidgeon?" Gooney Bird Greene said. "I have an idea."

9.

It was the day before Thanksgiving vacation —the day of the pageant. The school janitor, Lester Furillo, had used masking tape to attach the mural to the wall of the multipurpose room, and he had set up folding chairs for the audience. At the back of the large room, a table covered with a yellow paper tablecloth held two large platters of cupcakes and two pitchers of lemonade.

"These cupcakes are spectacular!" Mrs. Pidgeon had said when she opened the boxes that held them. "Look at this! Little turkeys and Pilgrim hats on the frosting! How did she ever do that, Gooney Bird?"

"She didn't do it," Gooney Bird replied. "You saw who brought them. You saw the name on the van. I think it's on the boxes too."

"Creative Catering," Beanie read from the lid of one box.

"I thought the room mother was supposed to make the cupcakes herself," Tricia said.

Gooney Bird shook her head. "I just told her to *provide* cupcakes. Remember the dialogue from when I told the story about getting the room mother? She asked what the room mother had to do, and I said provide cupcakes. You all know what *provide* means. We don't even need to get out our dictionaries."

"Well," Mrs. Pidgeon said as she arranged the cupcakes on a platter, "she certainly did a good job of providing, didn't she? But I wish she had brought them herself. I'd like to thank her."

"She's coming to the pageant," Gooney Bird assured her.

And now, in the afternoon, the guests were arriving. The second-graders were all in the small adjoining room, peeking out, watching the chairs in the multipurpose room fill up.

"There's my mom!" Tyrone said in an excited voice. "Lookit! She's got such a cool dress on!

"Mom!" he called. "I'm back here!" Tyrone's mother looked over with a grin and waved.

"Shhh!" the other children said. "Nobody's supposed to see us yet!"

"This is the dressing room!" Ben explained. "We're backstage! We have to be quiet. Hey!" he added. "Look! There's *my* mom!"

"My daddy came!" Keiko said, peeking out. "He must have closed the store for the afternoon! Look—there he is with my mom.

And see? That's my auntie! Hello, Oba-chan!"
she called, and a woman laughed and fluttered
her fingers in a wave.

Mrs. Pidgeon had been at the door of the
multipurpose room, greeting the guests. Now
she came back to where the children were
waiting. "I hear some giggling back here!" she
said with a smile.

"Are you all ready?" she asked. "We'll start
in a few minutes. Not quite everyone is here
yet. The room mother hasn't arrived."

"She said she might be a little late," Gooney Bird explained. "She said we could start
without her. Oh, look!" Gooney Bird pointed. "There's my mom! See? She's the one in
jeans, with a smiley face sweatshirt."

She wiggled her fingers in a wave, and her
mother waved back and took a seat.

There was a sudden commotion at the
door of the multipurpose room, and several
people got up from their seats to help. Malcolm looked, and groaned. "It's my mom," he

said, "with the triplets." He covered his eyes. "I'm not going to look," he said.

Mrs. Pidgeon put her arm around Malcolm. She and the other children watched while the janitor and several others helped to maneuver the huge triple stroller through the doorway.

"Are they asleep?" Malcolm asked, still hiding his eyes. "Please, please, could they be asleep?"

"Yes, they seem to be sleeping, Malcolm. It's okay. You can look. Don't worry," Mrs. Pidgeon told him. "We won't even mind if they wake up. We *like* babies."

"I love babies," whispered Felicia Ann. "I hope those triplets wake up so I can hold them."

"They always smell bad," Malcolm whispered back. He stuck out his tongue and crossed his eyes.

Mrs. Pidgeon went to the piano at the front of the multipurpose room and played a few chords to make people stop talking. It was what she did in the classroom, and it always worked there. It worked here too, with the grownups. They all became silent.

Mr. Leroy walked to the front of the room. The multipurpose room didn't have a stage. But he stood in front of the audience, wearing a necktie today with a plump turkey on it, and he spoke in a loud, clear voice, just the way Mrs. Pidgeon had told the children that they should.

The second-graders listened from behind the cracked-open door to their dressing room.

"Good afternoon, ladies and gentlemen," Mr. Leroy said. "I'm delighted to see so many parents here today, and some grandparents, I see, and even a few little brothers and sisters."

"And an auntie," whispered Keiko.

"Are your triplets brothers or sisters?" Felicia Ann asked Malcolm.

"Shhh," Malcolm said. "I'm not saying."

"And perhaps our new room mother as well?" Mr. Leroy said in a cheerful voice, looking around the audience. "Would the second-grade room mother like to stand?

"Maybe she's a little shy," he went on when no one stood. "But she certainly did provide wonderful refreshments, which we will enjoy after the performance.

"Speaking of the performance, I would like to mention that this is the fifth and final Thanksgiving pageant today. I watched the kindergarten children this morning—they did quite a lively dance during which they gobbled like turkeys and flapped imaginary wings. It was a little noisier than we had expected, but we got it under control after a bit, and I think we learned quite a bit about how dangerous wing-flapping can be, actually. For those of you who heard about it and are worried, incidentally, little Chloe McAllister is going to be fine. Nothing more than a fat lip."

Mr. Leroy straightened his tie. "After that," he went on, "the fourth grade performed quite an impressive play about Captain Miles Standish, who arrived on the *Mayflower,* and the great Indian Massasoit who became his friend.

"Unfortunately, Jason Carruthers and Jeffrey Hall, who were to play the roles of Miles Standish and Massasoit, are both absent today because there seems to be a stomach virus making the rounds. The other fourth graders, though, did a great job of explaining what the play would have been like if the leading characters had been available.

"Next, the first grade had worked very hard on learning all the words of the traditional Thanksgiving song 'We Gather Together,' and they sang it with remarkable enthusiasm for the audience. Unfortunately their teacher had not taken into account how difficult the lines *'He chastens and hastens his will to make known, The wicked oppressing now cease from distressing . . .'*

would be for people whose front teeth had recently fallen out, and I believe that was fourteen of the eighteen first-graders. But their gusto made up for their pronunciation.

"Then, finally, just an hour ago, we had the third grade's very colorful reenactment of the first Thanksgiving dinner. The third grade is so fortunate that one father provided large cardboard cartons, one for each performer to wear, with their heads of course emerging from the tops of the cartons, and each decorated as a type of food—squash, corn, potatoes, and the like. The third-graders got most of the way through a recitation and demonstration of the various courses of that dinner. I think, actually, that it might have been the food descriptions that brought on an onslaught of the stomach virus mid-performance, so that we had some unfortunate events, during which we had to extricate several children quickly from their cartons, and we ended up with a very slippery floor—"

"Both of the DeMarco twins threw up," Barry Tuckerman announced to the other children. "Identical throw-ups. I heard the janitor telling Muriel Holloway."

"Oh, no!" wailed Keiko.

"Shhh," Gooney Bird said.

"—but our hard-working custodian, Lester Furillo, has taken care of that," Mr. Leroy went on, "and with the help of some air-freshener I think we're in good shape for our final performance of the day from Mrs. Pidgeon's second grade.

"Thank you again for coming. I see someone else is just arriving. Is that another stroller?" He peered toward the back. "My goodness! So many vehicles today! Lester Furillo will help you in. There are still some seats in the back. Please make yourself comfortable." Mr. Leroy gestured toward the chairs in the back as more people entered. Then he turned to the piano and said, "Mrs. Pidgeon? It's all yours!"

Mrs. Pidgeon smiled. She played a verse of "We Gather Together" to call the crowd to attention and create a Thanksgiving mood. Then she nodded to Gooney Bird, who was in the doorway waiting for her cue to enter.

10.

While Mrs. Pidgeon played a rhythmic, drumming sort of music on the piano, Gooney Bird Greene danced from the door to the front of the multipurpose room. Her dance was a combination of shuffles, taps, and twirls, with an occasional pause for a hop. She was wearing fuzzy bedroom slippers, her long velvet skirt, a flowered Hawaiian shirt, and a top hat, onto which she had attached a blue feather.

The audience applauded at her entrance.

She ended her dance and bowed dramatically, steadying her hat with one hand.

"I am Squanto," Gooney Bird Greene announced.

"And these"—she gestured to the other children and they entered the room, marching, wearing their costumes of cardboard hats and headbands and belt buckles—"are Pilgrims and Native Americans.

"They are Squanto's friends," she added.

The Pilgrims and Native Americans stood in a semicircle behind Gooney Bird. They all adjusted their headgear and then stood with their hands at their sides, wiggling their eyebrows to hold up their hats and headbands, which were already slipping forward on their foreheads.

"Now, in honor of Thanksgiving, I am going to tell you a story," Gooney Bird said.

Mrs. Pidgeon played a "ta-DA" chord on the piano. The audience clapped and laughed. All of them knew already, because they had been told by their children, what a good storyteller Gooney Bird Greene was. Even Barbara Greene, Gooney Bird's mom, clapped and laughed.

From behind his headband, which had settled across his nose, Malcolm muttered, "I hope they don't clap too loud and wake up those triplets."

Gooney Bird took a few deep breaths, adjusted her posture, and began.

I am not the actual Squanto. The real Squanto was a Patuxet Indian who was born in a village near where the Pilgrims would land, but when he was born they hadn't landed yet.

He learned to speak English from some

early settlers. He helped them in many ways. He was a very helpful guy.

When some of them went back to England, they invited him to go along. His mother didn't want him to.

I can understand that. My mom wouldn't want me to go off to another country. She would say I was too young. We would probably have a big argument about it.

"Oops," Gooney Bird said. "That was an authorial intrusion. I didn't mean to do that. It's boring."

But he went anyway. This was way back in the 1600s. Squanto is dead now. I am not the real Squanto. I am an imitation.

"Mr. Leroy?" Gooney Bird said. "Could you tell us the meaning of *imitation*, please?"

The principal looked up and cleared his throat. "Well, ah," he said with a nervous little laugh. "It means *fake*. You are a fake Squanto."

Gooney Bird looked behind her at the semicircle of Pilgrims and Native Americans. "Barry?" she said. Barry, pushing his headband up on his forehead, stepped forward.

"*Imitation,*" Barry said in a loud voice. "*Something made to be as much as possible like something else.*" He bowed and stepped back. Everyone, including Mr. Leroy, clapped.

"Thank you, Barry," Gooney Bird said. To the audience, she explained, "Mrs. Pidgeon has taught us all to use a dictionary. We have gotten very good at it, for second-graders, because we didn't underestimate ourselves.

"*Underestimate?* Beanie?" Gooney Bird said.

Beanie stepped forward. She stumbled a bit, because her hat was over her eyes. Then she righted herself, stood straight, and said, "*Underestimate. To judge things as less than their real value.*" She curtsied, and whispered, "Like

I underestimated the bigness of my hat."

The audience laughed and clapped. Gooney Bird continued the story.

After a while, Squanto got tired of being in England. It was noisy and everybody went shopping all the time. He was homesick. So he cajoled a sea captain into taking him back to America.

"Felicia Ann," Gooney Bird announced. Felicia Ann, her Pilgrim bonnet completely covering her eyes and nose, stepped forward shyly.

"Cajole. To persuade someone to do something, by flattery or gentle argument," she said in her small voice.

The audience clapped. Gooney Bird continued.

He traveled around for a while, being helpful because he was a helpful guy. He was an interpreter between the Americans and the Indians—

"Malcolm?" Gooney Bird said. "*Inter-preter?*"

Malcolm unbent his green feather, straightened his headband, and wiggled his fingers the way he always did when he was nervous. He hesitated a moment, thinking. Then he said, "*Interpreter. Someone who translates something from one language to another and helps people understand each other.*"

The audience clapped.

"Shhh," Malcolm told them, with his fingers to his lips. "Don't clap too loud."

But suddenly—

The children smiled in anticipation at the *suddenly.*

—a bad ship captain tricked him into going onto his ship. It was a big scam. They made him a captive and took him to Spain. The captives all were sold as slaves. It made Squanto pretty mad.

But he was indefatigable.

Gooney Bird grinned. "Tyrone?" she said.

Tyrone, his headband completely covered in beads and with two feathers attached, strutted forward proudly. *"Indefatigable,"* he proclaimed. *"Never showing any sign of getting tired!"*

"Thank you, Tyrone," said Gooney Bird, after the applause. "I'm going to flash forward a bit now. That's a thing authors do."

After a long time Squanto finally made his way home. He had been away for years. And when he finally got home, he found that his village was gone. His people had all died. He was the last of his tribe.

It was very sad. But he became friends with the great chief Massasoit, and after a while he met the Pilgrims, who had just arrived. So he had some new friends and they hung out together.

The Pilgrims' lives in America would have been a fiasco if good Indians like Squanto had not helped them.

"Chelsea? *Fiasco?*"

Chelsea waved to her mother in the front row. *"Fiasco. A total failure."*

Chelsea curtsied, and gave a thumbs-up sign.

Gooney Bird finished her story.

Squanto had gotten lots of new clothes in England, and he had learned to dance.
The End.

Gooney Bird bowed, twirled in a circle, and did a small bit of hula.

"All of my story was absolutely true, except maybe the part about learning to dance, but I think he probably did," Gooney Bird said.

The audience rose to their feet, clapping and cheering. From the back of the room, when the applause quieted, the sound of babies crying came from the huge stroller. Malcolm pulled his headband down over his eyes and groaned.

"I have a couple more things to say," Gooney Bird announced. "The first Thanksgiving is a really good story because it tells about people becoming friends and being helpful to each other, and being thankful.

"So some of the second-graders want to say what they are thankful for. Nicholas?"

Nicholas said loudly, "The Muriel. I got to do the forest part. And Mrs. Pidgeon. She stretches our skills."

Next Gooney Bird said, "Keiko?"

"My family," Keiko said. "And Mrs. Pidgeon. She makes me smile."

"Ben?"

Ben hopped up and down. "My fixed broken arm." He held it up. "And Mrs. Pidgeon. I like her songs. And she lets us change socks."

"One more," Gooney Bird said, "and then we can have our refreshments. Malcolm?"

Malcolm sighed. Slowly he walked forward. He looked toward the big stroller. "Okay, I guess I'm thankful for my triplets," he said after a moment. "Their names are Taylor, Schuyler, and Tierney, and two are boys and one's a girl but I don't know which is which.

"And I'm thankful for Mrs. Pidgeon because she is very calm, even when I'm not.

"And I'm thankful for the room mother because she brought cupcakes, and I'm hungry."

From the back of the room, a voice called out. "I didn't *bring* them. I *provided* them. There is a difference!"

Then, very slowly, an elderly woman stood, lifting herself up by the arms of her wheelchair. Next to her, a nurse reached out to steady the chair.

"Here is what I'm thankful for," the old woman continued. "I'm thankful that Gooney Bird Greene called me on the telephone and asked me to be room mother. I haven't been room mother for thirty-five years. I was room mother when my daughter Patsy was in second grade. It was fun then, and it will be fun now.

"And mostly I am thankful that Patsy became a teacher. It makes me proud."

She lifted one hand and waved to Mrs. Pidgeon, seated at the piano. Mrs. Pidgeon dabbed her eyes with a hanky and then waved back. "Hi, Mom," she said with a smile.

"And don't forget, Gooney Bird Greene," the room mother said, "you promised me a special song."

Gooney Bird looked at Mrs. Pidgeon.

"Class?" Mrs. Pidgeon said, and played the first chord.

"Roooommmm Motherrrr," the children sang.

THE END

Gooney the Fabulous

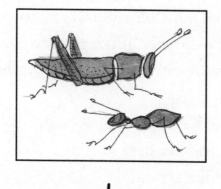

I.

"And so," Mrs. Pidgeon said, reading the final page of the book she was holding, "because the ant had worked very hard, he and his friends had food all winter. But the grasshopper had none, and found itself dying of hunger."

"Oh, no!" Keiko wailed. "I hate stories where people die!"

Malcolm, who had been rolling paper into balls while he listened to the story, tossed a little paper pellet at Keiko. "It's not people," he pointed out. "It's a dumb grasshopper! It's only a grasshopper! Just a grasshopper!"

"Nobody cares if a grasshopper dies!" Tyrone said.

"I do," Keiko murmured sadly. She folded her arms on her desk and then laid her head down on her arms.

"It's only a fable," Mrs. Pidgeon said. She held up the book. "*Aesop's Fables* is the title. Aesop was a man who lived a very long time ago. He was the creator of all of these fables. Tomorrow I'll read you another."

"Not about anybody dying!" Keiko implored, raising her head.

"No," Mrs. Pidgeon agreed. She leafed through the book. "I won't read 'The Wolf in Sheep's Clothing,' then, because I believe that one ends with the wolf eating the lamb—"

"Oh, noooo!" Keiko put her head back down and groaned.

"But I could read 'The Fox and the Grapes.' I think you'll enjoy that one, Keiko. You had some nice grapes in your lunch last week. I remember that you passed them around. That was very generous."

Keiko looked up and nodded. "Red seedless," she reminded everyone, "from my parents' grocery store. But Malcolm started a squishing contest, so I'm not bringing grapes ever again."

It was true. And unfortunately some of Mrs. Pidgeon's second-graders had joined in Malcolm's grape-squishing contest enthusiastically. Lester Furillo, the school custodian at the Watertower Elementary School, had had to come in during recess with his Shop-Vac to clean the floor of the multipurpose room where the children ate their lunch each day.

Mrs. Pidgeon placed the Aesop book upright, so the cover was visible, on top of the bookcase near the windows. "Time for social studies," she said. "But first, who would like to tell me what the moral is in 'The Ant and the Grasshopper'? Hands, please."

She looked around. "Barry Tuckerman?" As usual, Barry's hand was waving in the air.

"What's a moral?" Barry asked.

"My goodness," Mrs. Pidgeon said, "I should have explained that! Every fable has a moral. A moral is . . ." She hesitated.

Then she said, "Class, this is an opportunity to use our new dictionaries!"

She wrote the word on the board: MOR-AL.

The room was silent for a moment except for the sound of pages turning, as all the second-graders looked through the brand-new dictionaries that they had recently been given.

Gooney Bird Greene found it first and raised her hand. She was wearing fingerless gloves today, and a long flannel dress with a ruffle around the bottom; it looked suspiciously like a nightgown. Gooney Bird was known for her unusual outfits.

When Mrs. Pidgeon pointed to her, Gooney Bird stood and read aloud, "'A conclusion about how to behave, based on events in a story.'"

"Good dictionary work, Gooney Bird," said the teacher. "And so what was the moral of the fable about the ant and the grasshopper? What was the conclusion about how to behave?"

Gooney Bird rolled her eyes. "I could tell you," she said, "but I think it would be better if Malcolm did, because Malcolm is the one who *needs* advice on behavior!"

Mrs. Pidgeon chuckled. "Malcolm?" she said, pointing to him. He had the lid of his desk raised, and was shuffling the papers inside.

"What?" he asked, looking out from behind the raised lid.

"Could you tell us, please, what behavior we learned from the fable I just read?"

"Huh?"

Mrs. Pidgeon jiggled her knee. She always did that when she felt impatient. "Malcolm,"

she said, "I just read the class a story, a fable, actually, about a grasshopper and an ant. Maybe you didn't listen well. The ant worked very hard collecting and storing food, while the grasshopper just played and chirped. Then when winter came, the ant and his fellow ants all had plenty to eat, but the grasshopper—"

"Starved!" Keiko wailed. *"And died!"*

Tricia reached over and patted Keiko's back, to comfort her.

"So, Malcolm," Mrs. Pidgeon went on, "what do we learn from the story?"

Malcolm thought. "Don't step on ants," he said at last. "If ants are there, don't step on them. Never step on ants."

Mrs. Pidgeon sighed. She was silent for a long time. Everyone had noticed that Malcolm had recently begun saying everything three times. He couldn't seem to help it. They were all trying to ignore it, but sometimes it was difficult. The second-graders watched Mrs. Pidgeon. Finally she said, "Let's get out our social studies books, class. Turn to the chapter called 'Cities and Towns,' please."

"Wait!" called Malcolm. "I know! Clean up your crumbs after lunch or your kitchen will be full of ants! Don't leave your crumbs around! Wipe up any crumbs!"

"That's page thirty-two, class," Mrs. Pidgeon said. She held up the social studies book, open to a picture of a city filled with skyscrapers.

"Felicia Ann?" she said. "Did I see your hand up?"

Felicia Ann, looking at the floor, nodded. She was the shyest person in Mrs. Pidgeon's second grade. She never looked up. She rarely spoke above a whisper.

"Did you want to say something?" the teacher asked her.

"Yeth, pleathe," whispered Felicia Ann. She had recently lost her two front teeth.

"Listen, class," Mrs. Pidgeon said, and held

her finger in front of her mouth so that the children would be quiet.

"Work hard and don't play all the time," Felicia Ann said, blushing. "Plan ahead. Then you'll be ready for anything! A flood, or a blitherd—"

"What's a blitherd?" asked Beanie. "I never heard of a blitherd."

"She means blizzard," Gooney Bird explained.

"Yeth," Felicia Ann agreed. "Blitherd. And that'th the moral!" She looked up shyly and grinned.

"I liked the fable," she added, and looked at the floor again.

"Good," said Mrs. Pidgeon. "All right, class. Now we'll—"

"I don't get it!" Malcolm called out. "That story wasn't about floods or blizzards! It was insects! It was about insects! It was a story about insects! Ants! One time I was at my cousin's house and I sat on a whole hill of red ants, and—"

He was wiggling in his seat. Mrs. Pidgeon went to him and put her arm firmly across his shoulders. "Get a grip," she said. Sometimes she had to do that to calm Malcolm down. Sometimes Malcolm had to have a time-out. Malcolm had a hard time being calm at school, because at home his family had baby triplets and life was never calm. Their house, Malcolm said, was filled with the noise of babies crying, and their bathroom was filled with the smell of laundry, mostly in threes: three sets of baby clothes with spit-up on the front; and their kitchen was filled with groups of three bottles and three sippy cups and spilled milk and half-empty jars of strained peas, and sometimes Malcolm's mother announced, "I am going to scream three times!" and then she did, and after that she felt better for a while.

Now the class waited, as they were accustomed to doing, until Malcolm got a grip.

Then they took out their social studies books and turned to page 32.

All but Gooney Bird Greene. Her social studies book was on her desk, but she hadn't opened it.

"Mrs. Pidgeon?" Gooney Bird raised her hand, and when the teacher nodded to her, she said, "I have a great idea!"

The second-graders, including Malcolm, all cheered. Whenever Gooney Bird had a great idea, something exciting was about to happen.

2.

At lunchtime, in the multipurpose room, all of Mrs. Pidgeon's second-graders sat together and traded lunch parts, as they always did.

"Anyone want some of my sushi?" asked Gooney Bird Greene. "This one is called *kappa maki*. It's mostly cucumber." She held up a small glistening cylinder.

"What's that green stuff?" Barry asked, making a face.

"*Nori,*" Gooney Bird told him.

"That's seaweed," Keiko explained.

"Yuck," Barry replied.

"You shouldn't have told him it was sea-weed, Keiko," Gooney Bird said. "He might have thought it was spinach. Oh, well. I like it. I'll eat it myself." She popped the *kappa maki* into her mouth.

"Anyone want half a cream cheese and jel-ly on raisin bread?" Beanie asked. She held up a triangle of her sandwich.

"I'll take it, if the jelly isn't mooshing out," Chelsea said. "Let me see." She examined the sandwich half carefully. "Okay. I'll give you five carrot slices and an oatmeal cookie for it."

All around the table the second-graders made their trades. "YESSS!" Malcolm said suddenly. He was looking down at his lunch. "YESSS! YESSS!"

"Malcolm has all dessert!" Beanie pointed out. "How did you do that, Malcolm?"

He grinned happily at his pile of three cookies and three plastic cups of chocolate pudding. "Traded away two halves of an egg

salad sandwich and an apple," he explained, talking with his mouth full. "I traded——"

Gooney Bird interrupted him before he could describe it three times. "Where's your lunch, Nicholas?" Gooney Bird asked. Nicholas often brought KFC chicken pieces, and sometimes he let her trade for one.

"I gave it away," Nicholas said. He looked gloomy.

"Why?"

"I'm not hungry."

"Are you sick?" Gooney Bird asked sympathetically. "We could take you to the nurse's office."

"No, I'm okay," Nicholas said. But he put his head down in his arms, on the table.

Around them, the other classes were also eating and talking. It was December. Christmas, Hanukkah, and Kwanzaa decorations were on the walls. Mr. Leroy, the principal, had been wearing holiday neckties now for several days; today he was wearing one with small menorahs on it. Yesterday's had been reindeer. The kindergarten children had pasted photographs of themselves onto circles of construction paper and made a long chain of the dangling pictures that hung across the tops of the multipurpose room windows. The kitchen workers were all wearing Santa hats. And the school dog, a Saint Bernard named Bruno who belonged to Lester Furillo, the custodian, didn't seem to mind wearing plastic antlers. The whole school had a feeling of excitement because the holidays were coming.

"We need to make a sign," Beanie said, chewing on a carrot stick, "announcing the you-know-what."

Nicholas looked up briefly, then put his head back down.

"Yes! Our you-know-what!" Ben agreed. With a swat of his hand he flattened his empty milk carton.

"Our *fabulous* you-know-what!" added Chelsea as she wadded up her napkin and threw it, unsuccessfully, toward the trashcan.

The fabulous you-know-what was Gooney Bird's idea.

"We can write our own fables!" Gooney Bird had explained. "We already know how to write good stories—"

"Create interesting characters!" Ben announced.

"Describe them carefully so they seem real," Tricia added.

"Make them talk! That's called dialogue!" Barry called out.

"Put in a beginning, a middle, and an end," Tyrone said. Then he went into his rap routine. *"First you gotta start 'cuz you gotta have heart, and next you gotta middle 'cuz you feelin' like a fiddle, and when you gonna end everybody be yo' friend*—" He stood at his desk and moved his body.

"Go, Tyroooonnne!" Malcolm called. "Go! Go!"

Mrs. Pidgeon, smiling, went to Tyrone and placed her arm firmly over his shoulders. "You're good, Tyrone. You're really good! But save it till recess. Class, quiet down, please."

When the room was silent, Felicia Ann looked up and spoke in her shy, whispery voice. "And alwayth put in a thuddenly," she reminded the class.

"Suddenly," Mrs. Pidgeon announced, "I think we have an interesting project, compliments of Gooney Bird Greene!"

"Yay!" the second-graders shouted, and Gooney Bird, holding her long maybe-a-nightgown out to the sides, curtsied politely.

With the teacher's help, the class decided that the fable project would become, also, a holiday celebration for the school. They had time, they thought. There were still two weeks before vacation.

Each child would write a fable, an animal story, using an animal that matched his or her own initial.

"I could be a bull! B is for bull!" Ben called out, making horns out of his hands and leaning forward with a snort. He pawed the floor with one foot.

"I could be a tiger!" shouted Tyrone.

"Remember, though, each fable must have a moral!" Mrs. Pidgeon reminded them. "And a moral is what?"

They were all silent for a moment. Then Beanie raised her hand. "It's when you learn how to behave, from the story. I mean, from the fable."

"Good for you, Beanie. All right, class. Be thinking about choosing your animal and creating your fable and its moral. And then, after we listen to your fables here in the classroom—"

She interrupted herself. "Nicholas? Is something wrong?"

Nicholas had his head down on his desk. He raised it slightly. "No," he said.

"Mrs. Pidgeon! Mrs. Pidgeon!" Chelsea was waving her hand in the air.

Mrs. Pidgeon nodded to her. "Yes, Chelsea?"

"Can we wear costumes? For our animals?"

The teacher hesitated. "We don't really have time for making elaborate costumes, I'm afraid. Remember what a mess it turned into at Thanksgiving, with all those Pilgrims and Native Americans?"

The class looked disappointed.

"I have an idea," Gooney Bird, who was still standing after her curtsey, said. "We don't need whole costumes. But just one little thing, to show the animal. Like if Ben's fable was about a bull, he could wear, oh, maybe a *tail* . . ."

All of the children shrieked with laughter. *"Ben's got a ta-il, Ben's got a ta-il,"* Malcolm called in a singsong voice. *"Ben's got a —"*

"I'm not being a bull," Ben said angrily. "I changed my mind. My fable's going to be about some other animal."

"Let's each keep our animal secret for now," Mrs. Pidgeon suggested. "Then, when our fables are ready, we can wear one thing —not a large thing—to indicate something about the animal. It doesn't have to be a tail," she added, looking at Ben.

"Will you do one, Mrs. Pidgeon?" Keiko asked.

"Certainly I will. I'm part of this class."

"You could be a pigeon!" Barry pointed out. "Can a bird be in a fable?"

"Of course," the teacher said. "Aesop wrote one about a crow.

"All of you start thinking. Right now we must turn to our social studies. But be thinking about your fables. And after they are all finished, on the last day of school before vacation, we can share them with the rest of the school by having a parade through the halls!"

"A parade of the animals!" Keiko said, and clapped her hands.

"A Fabulous Parade!" said Gooney Bird Greene.

3.

"Gooney Bird," suggested Mrs. Pidgeon, "I'm going to put you in charge of this, since it was your wonderful idea. Most of the children are ready. So would you come here to the front of the class and call on them?"

A week had passed. Now, with just one week left until vacation, the second-graders had been working with excitement on the project. Many of them had brought in their costume parts and were eager to display them and tell their fables.

Gooney Bird, who always looked as if

she were wearing a costume even when she wasn't, came to the front of the classroom. Today she was wearing her hiking boots; two different-colored knee socks, one blue and one yellow, appeared at the top of the boots. Even though there was snow on the ground outdoors, Gooney Bird was wearing red plaid Bermuda shorts. She also wore a short-sleeved T-shirt in army camouflage colors, and dangling around her neck was a sparkly rhinestone necklace.

Mrs. Pidgeon went to sit in her desk chair. Then she said, "Actually, Gooney Bird, maybe you'd like to go first, since it was your idea?"

Gooney Bird thought for a moment. Then she said, "No. I want to go last."

"All right then, you may go last. Time to choose who goes first!"

"Volunteers?" Gooney Bird asked, looking around the classroom. "Hands?"

Many hands shot into the air. Barry Tuckerman, as always, was half standing at his desk, waving his arm wildly. Felicia Ann, as always, was looking at the floor. But her hand was raised in a timid sort of way.

Gooney Bird looked at Nicholas. "Nicholas," she said, "you didn't raise your hand. But would you like to be first?"

Nicholas, who had been looking gloomy all week, shook his head.

"Is there anything we can do to make you feel more cheerful?" Gooney Bird asked in a kindly voice.

"No," Nicholas muttered.

"Well, then." Gooney Bird looked around the room at all the waving hands. Finally she looked at the teacher's desk. "Mrs. Pidgeon," she asked, "is your fable ready?"

"Yes," said Mrs. Pidgeon. "I have it right here."

"And your costume?" asked Gooney Bird.

Mrs. Pidgeon nodded.

"I'd like you to go first, then. You're a member of this class, after all."

Mrs. Pidgeon smiled. "All right," she said. She stood up. She was wearing black slacks and a black turtleneck shirt. She reached into the bag that she had stored under her desk and brought out a white vest and put it on.

"How shall we do this, Gooney Bird?" she asked. "Would it be fun to have the class guess what animal each of us is?"

"*No,*" Nicholas said loudly.

It was very startling. Nicholas ordinarily was a cheerful, outgoing boy. But all week he had been acting strangely.

Gooney Bird decided to ignore him. "Yes," she said, "let's guess. Class, take a look at Mrs. Pidgeon and guess what animal she is! Remember, it must begin with a P!"

"But P is for her *last* name," Tricia pointed out.

Mrs. Pidgeon laughed. "That's true," she said. "But my first name is Patsy! I'm a two-P person! Now see if you can guess my animal."

The class all looked carefully. Mrs. Pidgeon was entirely black except for her white middle.

"*Penguin!*" the children all shouted.

"I saw *March of the Penguins!*" Beanie called out.

"Me too!" Malcolm said. "I did too! I saw it too! I saw *March of the Penguins!*"

"So did I!" called Ben. "My dad took me!"

"I saw it!" Chelsea said loudly.

"I thaw it too," Felicia Ann whispered, "but it wath tho thad!"

"Shhhhh," Gooney Bird said, and she held her finger in front of her mouth. "I'm sure Mrs. Pidgeon's fable won't be sad. Will it, Mrs. Pidgeon?" Gooney Bird stepped aside so that the teacher could stand at the front of the class to read her fable.

Mrs. Pidgeon was laughing. "No," she said, "it isn't sad at all. But it also isn't about a penguin!"

"It isn't?" asked Gooney Bird, looking puzzled.

"No. I'm going to write the name of my animal on the board. I'm afraid guessing is not going to be a good idea. It might take forever. Instead, each of us can write our animal in a list. I'll start right here." Mrs. Pidgeon picked up the chalk and held it to the board. "Then, after we're all done," she said, "we can have a lesson in alphabetizing. Remember my beginning letter, P?"

She wrote an uppercase P on the board.

Then she added an A, an N, a D, and another A.

"Panda!" the class called out. They looked at their teacher again. Her arms and legs were black, and her middle was white. A perfect panda.

"Now," Mrs. Pidgeon said, "I'll read my fable."

Once there was a small panda who lived in a bamboo grove in China. He was a happy panda who spent his days playing in the tall stalks of bamboo and nibbling at the leaves.

One day a majestic deer wandered into the bamboo grove.

"Hello," said the deer to the panda. "You look as if you are enjoying your nibbling."

"Yes," the panda replied. "I am."

"I myself prefer to eat the tips of rhododendrons," the deer said. "They are quite yummy, and I think they have a lot of vitamins."

"Bamboo is yummy, too," said the panda, "but I'd be happy to give a rhododendron a try, on your recommendation."

So the majestic deer led the small panda out of the bamboo grove and through a meadow, then to a rhododendron bush at the edge of the woods.

"Here," said the deer. "Help yourself."

The panda nibbled curiously. The taste was not bad. It was very different from bamboo leaves. He ate several twigs and a few blossoms.

But suddenly his stomach began to hurt. He felt sick.

"I think I want to go home now," he called out to the deer. But the deer had gone away. The panda was alone, and lost.

With a badly aching stomach, and crying a bit because he was frightened, the panda found his way with much difficulty back to the bamboo grove.

He made himself comfy there and decided never to leave the bamboo grove again.

"That's the end," Mrs. Pidgeon said. She folded her paper, placed it on her desk, and smiled at the class.

"It wath a good fable," Felicia Ann said.

"Not too scary," Keiko added. "Just a little scary, at the *suddenly* part, when his stomach hurt. But *suddenly*s are almost always a little scary."

"Nicholas?" Mrs. Pidgeon said. "Did you enjoy it?"

Nicholas lifted his head briefly. "It was okay," he muttered.

"Thank you, Mrs. Pidgeon. You may take your seat," Gooney Bird said. She was very good at being in charge.

"Now, class," she went on, "who can tell the moral of Mrs. Pidgeon's panda fable?"

All of the children were silent, thinking of the story of the panda. "Put on your thinking caps," Gooney Bird reminded them.

Malcolm's hand shot up. "I know!" he called out. "I know what it is! Oh, I know—"

"Malcolm?" Gooney Bird pointed to him. "Would you tell us the moral? And by the way, you only need to say it one time."

Malcolm stood up at his desk. "Don't ever, ever go off with some stranger who offers you candy!" he announced loudly. "Remember not to go—"

"*Thtranger danger,*" Felicia Ann murmured, interrupting Malcolm.

"Oh dear," Keiko said. "That's scary."

Mrs. Pidgeon stood up. "That's a good reminder, Malcolm. But it's not exactly the moral I was thinking of. I'm going to tell you my fable's moral so that you'll all get the hang of it.

"The moral of the panda fable is this: *Sometimes what you already have is the best thing.*"

The children were silent for a moment, thinking it over.

"I get it!" Ben said. "Like when I got new hockey skates, but my old ones were really more comfortable!"

"And when my dad got his new car?" Chelsea added. "He said he really liked the old one better even though it had a hundred million miles on it!"

"And my mom and dad!" Malcolm called. "They already had *me!* I was already their kid! They'd had me for seven years! But then they got—"

Mrs. Pidgeon went to Malcolm and put her hand on his shoulder. At the same time she reached with her other hand to Nicholas, and rubbed his back in a comforting way. Nicholas didn't look up.

"Gooney Bird," Mrs. Pidgeon said, "we have a lot of fables to get through. How about calling on the next person?"

Gooney Bird nodded, and looked around the room.

"Keiko?" she said. "You next."

4.

Keiko stood. She reached under her desk, picked up a pink canvas backpack, and put her arms through the straps. But she did it backwards, so that the pack was suspended against her chest. Then she walked to the front of the classroom.

The class began to laugh. "I know!" "I get it!" they called out.

Keiko went to the board, and under PAN-DA, in her best uppercase printing, she wrote:
KANGAROO

Then she turned to the class, unfolded her paper, and announced, "My fable is called—"

She interrupted herself and looked over at Mrs. Pidgeon and at Gooney Bird, who was standing beside the teacher's desk. "Are we supposed to have a title?" she asked.

"Oh, yes," Gooney Bird said. "All stories have titles."

"But Mrs. Pidgeon's fable didn't have a title!" Chelsea called.

"Uh-oh," said Mrs. Pidgeon. "I forgot. And Gooney Bird is right; all stories should have titles. See? Not even teachers are perfect!"

The second-graders, all but Nicholas, laughed.

"Of course, they are *almost* perfect," Mrs. Pidgeon added, and the class, all but Nicholas, laughed again.

"The title of my fable," Mrs. Pidgeon said, "was, ah, 'The Panda in the Bamboo Grove.' But now it's Keiko's turn. Go on, Keiko."

Keiko nodded and began again. "The title of my fable is 'The Kangaroo Who Came Home.'"

Once a very small kangaroo hopped out of his mother's pouch and went off to play.

He played with a koala and a dingo and a wallaby. They played tag and hide-and-seek.

Then it got late. It was time for supper. The animal friends said goodbye to each other and started for their homes.

But the baby kangaroo could not find his home! He had not been watching. His mother had hopped away across the dry land through the scratchy grass. He could not see her anymore. He did not know where she had gone.

He began to cry.

The koala said, "Come with me to my eucalyptus tree. You can share my dinner and sleep in my tree tonight."

So the kangaroo went with the koala. But

he couldn't climb like the koala, and the tree was full of sharp twigs. It was very uncomfortable, and he did not like the taste of eucalyptus at *all*.

So he cried again.

The dingo said, "Come with me. I live in a small cave in those rocks over there. You can share my dinner and sleep in my cave."

The kangaroo tried that. But the dingo was eating rabbit for dinner, and the kangaroo was a vegetarian. He couldn't eat rabbit. And the cave was cold, not comfy and warm like his mother's pouch.

So he cried again.

The wallaby said, "Well, I can take you to where I live. As you know, I am a kind of kangaroo myself, so I eat leaves and roots the way you do. But I'm afraid there is no room in my mother's pouch for an extra. You will have to sleep on the ground, and it will not be cozy."

The little kangaroo cried and cried.

Suddenly he heard a thumping sound. He looked up. It was his own mother, leaping with her strong legs and big feet toward him. She had been looking everywhere.

He hopped to her and right into her pouch, which was warm and snug. There was milk waiting for him.

His mother scolded him gently and he promised never to wander away again, at least not until he was big.

Then he went happily to sleep.

"That's the end," Keiko said. "Did you like it?"

The second-graders clapped. They had liked her fable very much.

"It was a happy *suddenly*, when he heard his mom coming," Beanie pointed out, "not a scary one."

"Yes," Keiko said. "I wouldn't put in anything scary."

"Happy *suddenly*s are just fine," Gooney Bird told the students. "I think I may put one into *my* fable, actually. Thank you for that idea, Keiko."

She looked around. "Now," she said, "thinking caps! Who would like to tell us what the moral is? What kind of behavior are we supposed to learn from Keiko's fable?"

"Tricia?" Gooney Bird pointed to Tricia.

"Be a vegetarian!" Tricia said. "That's the moral!"

"My Aunt Carol is a vegetarian!" Barry called out. "My dad says she's a nutcase!"

"My mom's cousin Phyllis is a vegetarian!" shouted Chelsea. "And my mom says yeah, eat your dumb pumpkin casserole and more turkey for *us* at Thanksgiving!"

Mrs. Pidgeon stood up. "Class," she said, "many people are vegetarians. Nothing wrong with that. But I don't think that was the moral of the fable, was it, Keiko?"

Keiko shook her head. "No. And anyway, I like hot dogs."

"I have a feeling," Mrs. Pidgeon said, "that the moral of Keiko's fable is the same thing that we all remember from a certain movie. A movie that had a scarecrow and a tin man in it."

"*The Withard of Oth,*" whispered Felicia Ann.

"I know!" Malcolm shrieked. "I know! Call on me! I know!"

"I'm going to call first on Nicholas, I think," Mrs. Pidgeon said.

Nicholas looked up. He frowned. But he gave the answer. *"There's no place like home,"* he said.

"Correct! And you know what?" Gooney Bird said. "In the movie, Dorothy says it three times! So we should have let Malcolm give the answer!"

"Go, Malcolm!" shouted Tyrone.

"There's no place like home! There's no

place like home! There's no place like home!" Malcolm called out, with a big smile.

Then his smile changed to a scowl, and he added, "Unless the home has triplets."

5.

Beanie went to the front of the classroom to present her fable next. First she reached into her backpack and took out a small stuffed bear.

"This isn't really a costume, I guess," she said, "because I'm not *wearing* it. But my fable is about a bear, so I brought my old bear from home. I got him when I was born. His name is Teddy."

"That's a baby thing, to have a teddy bear when you're in second grade!" Barry said.

The class fell silent. Beanie looked embarrassed.

"Children?" Mrs. Pidgeon said, and she
stood up. "When I was a very little girl, I had
a stuffed lamb. I used to sleep with him. His
name was Fleecy. And you know what?"

"What?" the class asked.

"I still have him. I don't sleep with him
anymore. But Fleecy sits on a shelf in my
bedroom, and I still love him just as much as
I did all those years ago."

"I have a bear," Tricia said. "I call mine
Bear-Bear."

"Tho do I," Felicia Ann whispered. "I
thleep with my bear."

"I have a doll," Keiko said. "Not a bear. A
soft doll with a painted face, and she is so old
that her face is almost worn away, but I still
love her just as much."

"I have a bunny," Ben said. "When I was
born everybody gave me bunnies because of

the story of Benjamin Bunny. My mom said I got eight bunnies when I was born. I only have one left, but I sleep with him every night, and when we went to visit my cousins and I forgot Bunny, I couldn't sleep."

Tyrone stood up. "Mine's a clown," he said. "My Nana made it. *Got me a clown and he never makes a frown, makes me laugh as much as a giraffe—*"

The class began to rap with Tyrone. *"Got me a clown—"*

"Enough," Mrs. Pidgeon said, laughing. "You'll get your turn, Tyrone, when you present your fable. But for now we want to hear Beanie's. And also, Barry?"

"What?"

"It isn't a baby thing at all, to have a bear. Or a lamb, or a doll, or a clown. I'd like you to apologize to Beanie."

"Sorry, Beanie," Barry said.

"That's okay." Still holding Teddy, Beanie turned and wrote BEAR on the list, just be-

low KANGAROO. Then she unfolded her paper and read the title of her fable.

The Very Small Bear

Barry interrupted her. "Actually," Barry admitted, "I have a stuffed walrus, and his tusks are all gross because I suck on them."

Mrs. Pidgeon put her finger to her mouth. "Shhhh," she said to Barry. "Let's be good listeners."

Once there was a mother bear with twin cubs. One was a big strong bear cub, and very brave. But the other was quite small and weak, and frightened of things.

When they went to the river so their mom could teach them to get fish, the big cub jumped right in and splashed around. He grabbed a salmon with his claws. But the little cub was afraid of the water, and he cried. "It's cold!" he said. "And I can't swim!"

The big cub made fun of the little one. "Sissy!" the bigger cub said, and grabbed another fish for himself.

When their mom took them to the orchard where sometimes she stole apples from the farmer's trees, the big cub jumped right up into a tree and grabbed apples and ate them with a gulp.

But the little cub only peeked out from his hiding place behind the corner of the barn. "What if the farmer sees us?" he said. "What if the farmer has a gun and *shoots* us?" It made him shake with fear just to think about it.

"Scaredy-cat!" said the big cub to his brother, and he stuffed another apple into his own mouth.

The mother bear took them to a dead tree she knew of where she could get honey from a hive inside the trunk.

"Yay!" said the big cub. "Honey!" He climbed up the trunk of the tree, reached inside, and brought out his paw coated with sticky, delicious honey. The bees buzzed around angrily but he didn't care.

The little bear hid in the bushes and watched. He was very scared of bees. "What if they sting my nose?" he said.

So the big cub got bigger and bigger and healthier and healthier, but the little cub was always skinny and scared.

Beanie looked up. "That's the end," she said. "But it doesn't have a *suddenly*. And I don't think it has a moral, either."

Gooney Bird took the paper from Beanie and looked at it carefully. "You know what?" she said. "I don't think that was the end."

"It isn't?" Beanie said.

"You just stopped too soon," Gooney Bird pointed out.

"What if, after this last sentence—'the little cub was always skinny and scared'—you then added a *suddenly*?"

"But what could it say after that?" Beanie asked.

"Class?" Gooney Bird turned to the second-graders, who were all listening and thinking. "Ideas?"

Malcolm shouted, "Suddenly the big cub was killed by a lion and the little one got to eat all his food! This big lion comes and kills him, see! How about if a lion—"

"Oh, *no!*" wailed Keiko.

"Other ideas?" Gooney Bird asked.

"I have one," said Felicia Ann timidly.

"Remember, it should start with a *suddenly*," Gooney Bird reminded her.

Felicia Ann nodded. "Thuddenly," she said, "the big cub got thtuck in a bear trap! He wath too fat to get out!"

"And then what?"

"Well, hith little brother came along and wath able to reach in and help him, becuth he wath thkinny! He unlocked the trap and let hith brother out!"

"YES!" called Tyrone. *"Caught in a trap 'cuz you acted like a sap, and along come your bro and help to let you go—"*

"Tyrone," said Mrs. Pidgeon, with a meaningful look.

"Sorry," Tyrone said.

"What do you think of Felicia Ann's suggestion?" Gooney Bird asked Beanie.

Beanie nodded happily. "I like it! And it has a moral!" she said.

"What's the moral?"

"Be nice to your brother!" Malcolm called out. "Always share with your brother! Your brother is—"

Mrs. Pidgeon put her hand firmly on Malcolm's shoulder. "Let Beanie answer," she said.

"Well," Beanie said slowly. *"Everybody has things they can do. You don't have to be big or brave. The important thing is to be helpful."*

"Sounds good to me!" Gooney Bird said. "Class? What do you think?"

"Sounds good!" the class said.

"The bear didn't die in the trap, did he?" Keiko asked fearfully.

"No," Beanie said. "He came out of the trap and went and got some fish and other stuff for his brother, to say thank you.

"The end," Beanie added.

6.

Felicia Ann went next.

"My fable ith very, very short," she said apologetically when she went to the front of the class.

"That's all right," Gooney Bird told her.

"You'll thee why," Felicia Ann said.

She was wearing a bright pink dress and matching pink tights. She went to the board. Carefully she printed, under BEAR, the word FLAMINGO.

Then Felicia Ann turned to the class and

unfolded her paper. They could all see the very short sentences printed neatly on it.

"The title ith 'The Fable of the Flamingo,'" Felicia Ann read aloud.

Oneth there wath a flamingo. It didn't mind being bright pink.

But itth legs were pink, too. And that made it embarrathed. The flamingo thought that itth legth should be brown, like other birds' legth.

Tho it tried to hide them. It pulled one leg up to itth tummy in a folded way tho that no one would thee it.

But thuddenly, when it pulled the other leg up, it fell over.

Tho it only hid one leg at a time.

And it had a very hard time walking.

The end.

Everyone noticed that Felicia Ann was wobbling a bit. She had read her fable standing on one leg, with the other leg tucked up as high as possible.

After she read "The end," she sighed with relief and put her leg down.

"I almotht tipped over," she said, "tho it had to be short."

"It was a good fable, though," Gooney Bird told her. "Class? Didn't you think so?"

The other second-graders, all but Nicholas, who was scribbling aimlessly on a piece of paper, nodded.

"And the moral?" Gooney Bird asked. "Do you want the class to guess, or would you like to tell us?"

"I'll tell the moral," Felicia Ann said shyly. "It'th thith: *You should be very proud of what color you are.*"

The class cheered and clapped.

"Even your legth," Felicia Ann added. She grinned. Then she went back to her desk.

Mrs. Pidgeon stood up. "Class," she said, "we have time for just one more fable before lunch, and then we'll do some more tomorrow.

"Nicholas?" she asked. "Would you like to be the final fable today?"

But Nicholas, looking miserable, shook his head no.

"Well," Mrs. Pidgeon said, "I can see that three of you—Chelsea, Malcolm, and Tyrone—are eager to have a turn. I wish you'd raise your hands with that much enthusiasm during math!

"Let's see. What do you think, Gooney Bird?"

"Well," Gooney Bird said, looking at the list on the board, "we've had three girls already today. So we should give a boy a turn."

Chelsea groaned and stopped waving her hand.

"And," Gooney Bird went on, "we've all been sitting and we probably could use the exercise. So let's let Tyrone do his. And let's all stand up for it.

"You too, Nicholas," Gooney Bird added, after the class had stood up but Nicholas was still slumped at his desk. Grudgingly, Nicholas stood.

With a grin Tyrone made his way to the front of the room. He carried no paper, but he had a shiny pie tin in his hand, and when he reached the front of the room, he hung the pie tin, which had a string attached to it in two places, around his neck.

"My fable is—" he began, his sneakers already tapping on the floor.

"Write your animal on the board!" Chelsea called. But Tyrone only grinned and moved his feet.

"Go ahead and yell it but I dunno how to spell it," he chanted, *"can't write it on the list 'cuz my spelling might be dissed, so I tell the story 'bout it and if you wanna you can shout it . . ."*

The whole class began to tap their feet

and hum along with Tyrone. Even Nicholas looked up with interest.

The Tale of Tyrannosaurus Rex

You got it, it be TEEEE REX, TEEEE REX—okay for you to shout it 'cuz there ain't no way about it—this creature, he come along and he be so strong, sooo strong . . .

Tyrone twirled around and came to a stop, his pie tin dangling and bouncing on his chest.

. . . he got armor plates so no enemy can bite him, and he never gets in fights 'cuz everybody scared to fight him, and he taller than the trees and he never gets no fleas, and he don't say thank you and he don't say please, 'cuz he rule the earth since his mama give him birth . . .

"Lemme hear it!" Tyrone said, and the class, accustomed by now to his style, repeated the words. "Since his mama give him birth, since his mama give him birth . . ."

There was a brief knock at the classroom door. It opened, and Mr. Leroy, the principal, appeared. He was wearing a tie that had candy canes on it, and some holly berries. "I heard some strange sounds from this classroom," he said, smiling, "and I suspected that the famous Tyrone was performing. May I sit in?"

He tiptoed over and sat down at Tyrone's empty desk. Mr. Leroy was a tall man, and sitting at a child's desk made his legs fold in an odd way, with his knees sticking up, but he never seemed to mind.

"It's a fable," Tricia whispered to him from the next desk. "Tyrone's doing a fable."

Tyrone continued.

Mr. Leroy don't be bitter, gonna hear about this critter, Teeee rex, Teeee rex . . .

"Teeee rex, Teeee rex," the class chanted. Mrs. Pidgeon and Mr. Leroy joined in.

He be one huge dude, every minute needin' food, and he's chompin' up the scene, eatin' everything that's green . . .

Tyrone danced across the open space at the front of the room, grabbing at imaginary things with his teeth, imitating a large animal grazing. "Lemme *hear* it!" he called, and the class, and Mrs. Pidgeon, and Mr. Leroy all chanted with him:

"Everything that's green, everything that's green!"

Then Tyrone stopped dancing, stood still, and lowered his voice to finish his fable.

Big T. rex, he rule the earth and he rule the moon, but he be in trouble really soon, 'cuz one fine day as quick as a wink, he go to wake up and he now extinct.

EXXXXXTINCT!

Tyrone bowed while the class clapped and cheered, as they always did for Tyrone's performances. Mrs. Pidgeon, laughing, said, "Great as always, Tyrone. But haven't you forgotten something? What does a fable always have?"

"Gettin' to that," Tyrone explained. He turned to the class. "Wanna hear a moral?"

They nodded.

"I can't *hear* you!" Tyrone called. "Wanna hear a moral?"

"Wanna hear a moral!" the class chanted.

"Louder!"

"WANNA HEAR A MORAL!"

Tyrone resumed his position, tapped his feet, and finished his rap.

Big be nice, and big be cool, but big don't mean that you gonna rule, 'cuz here's the moral of ol' T. rex: *BIG MEAN NUTHIN' IF YOU DON'T DO SCHOOL!*

"School! School!" the class repeated, chanting and clapping.

"Well," said Mr. Leroy as he unfolded his long legs and stood up, "thank you, Tyrone. That made my day.

"Made my day," the principal chanted, dancing toward the door. "Made my day. *Big mean nuthin' if you don't do school.*" He disappeared, still chanting, into the hall.

Mrs. Pidgeon went to the board and wrote TYRANNOSAURUS REX below FLAMINGO. "Now: lunchtime, class," she said with a smile.

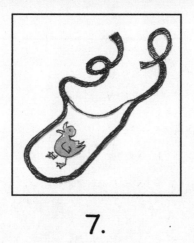

7.

"Mrs. Pidgeon?" Tricia asked the teacher at lunch. Sometimes the teachers all sat together at a separate table, or even ate their lunch in the teachers' room. But today Mrs. Pidgeon was eating with the children. She had even made a trade, and given Gooney Bird a nice red apple in exchange for the five olives-stuffed-with-anchovy that Gooney Bird had brought as an hors d'oeuvre.

"I think lunch ought to have courses," Gooney Bird always said. "I like to have an appetizer—sometimes I call it the hors

d'oeuvre—and a salad, and an entrée, and a dessert course. I'd do a soup course, too, but every time I've tried it, my soup has spilled before lunchtime. And I do hate it when my dessert gets wet."

Today Gooney Bird, to everyone's amazement, had taken something made of embroidered cloth out of her lunchbox. She unfolded it carefully and tied it around her neck.

"That's a bib!" Malcolm bellowed. "That's what babies wear! Babies wear bibs!"

"I know that," Gooney Bird replied calmly. "Actually, I bought this one in the baby section of the Goodwill store."

"But why would you wear a baby thing?" Beanie asked.

"It's sensible," Gooney Bird replied. "Babies wear bibs to keep their clothes clean. That's a sensible thing to do. I am a sensible person. So I have decided to wear a bib." She smoothed the bib over her chest. It had an embroidered duck on it.

"But aren't you embarrathed?" Felicia Ann whispered.

"I am never ever embarrassed," Gooney Bird replied.

Everyone was silent for a moment. Then Malcolm said, "We have a whole lot of bibs at home. A million bibs. We have—"

Mrs. Pidgeon interrupted him in a kindly way. "Time to eat, Malcolm," she said gently. Then she turned to Tricia. "Did you want to ask me something? I think we all got distracted by Gooney Bird's bib."

Tricia nodded. "Me and Ben—" she began. Then she stopped. Mrs. Pidgeon had held up a finger—she called it her grammar finger—as a reminder.

"Ben and I," Tricia corrected.

"Good. That is much better grammar," Mrs. Pidgeon explained.

"How come Tyrone can use bad grammar when he raps?" Malcolm asked. "And you never once hold up your grammar finger?"

"Ahhh," Mrs. Pidgeon said with a chuckle. "Good question, Malcolm. Rap is a special art form. And it uses a different grammar. So Tyrone can say, in a rap—well, give us an example, Tyrone, would you?"

Tyrone looked down at his lunch, a pear and a sandwich on a paper napkin in front of him. He thought for a moment, then chanted, "Ain't no pear as big as my hair, 'cuz pears be small and my hair be tall . . ."

Mrs. Pidgeon laughed. "All right," she said. "Now, Tyrone, tell us that in proper grammar."

Tyrone grinned. Then he said, "There isn't any pear as big as my hair, because pears are small, but I always comb my hair up to make it look pretty large."

"See the difference?" Mrs. Pidgeon asked, and the children nodded.

"So: what were you going to ask me, Tricia? About you and Ben?"

"Is it okay if Ben and I do our fable together?"

"Certainly."

"Because we were talking about our initials, and Ben was going to do BEAR, but Beanie already did. But we thought of a fable you already read to us, by Aesop—"

"Which one?" Mrs. Pidgeon asked.

"'The Tortoise and the Hare,'" Tricia said.

All of the children nodded. "I remember that one!" Keiko said. "I liked that one."

"But there's no B animal in it!" Chelsea pointed out. "Tortoise. Hare. T and H."

Ben explained. "We're going to make it 'The Tortoise and the Bunny.' T and B for Tricia and Ben."

"Bunny!" shrieked Chelsea. "Ben's going to be a *bunny!*"

"*Bunny*'s a baby word!" Malcolm said, sputtering with laughter. "Babies say 'bunny'! Bunny is—"

Mrs. Pidgeon put her calm-down hand on his shoulder. "But a minute ago," she said, "we were talking about bibs. Bibs can be called baby things. But look at Gooney Bird."

Everyone looked. Gooney Bird was still wearing her bib with the embroidered duck on it. "I have another bib at home," Gooney Bird said, "and I'll wear it tomorrow. It features a bunny."

"Good," Mrs. Pidgeon said. "And tomorrow Tricia and Ben can do their fable, 'The Tortoise and the Bunny.'"

"I am never ever embarrassed," Ben said proudly.

Walking back to the classroom after lunch, Nicholas trudged slowly, dragging his feet. The other children hurried ahead, all but Gooney Bird. She walked beside Nicholas. Mrs. Pidgeon, walking slowly too, took his hand.

"Nicholas," Mrs. Pidgeon said softly, "do

you want to tell Gooney Bird and me what is wrong?"

Nicholas shook his head. But now they could see that there were tears on his cheeks.

Mrs. Pidgeon called to the rest of the children. "Go on into the classroom," she said, "and start studying your spelling words! I'll be there in a minute."

She knelt beside Nicholas. "You know," Mrs. Pidgeon said, "every single person has something that they feel upset about. It's one of the reasons that we read fables. They teach us about things."

Nicholas sniffled. He looked at the floor.

"For example, I know there are some children in my second grade who think they don't like school, and it isn't important.

"But Tyrone's fable about the T. rex had a moral, remember?"

Nicholas didn't look up. But he was listening. He shook his head.

"Gooney Bird? Do it with me?" Mrs.

Pidgeon asked. Then she and Gooney Bird chanted together, *"Big mean nuthin' if you don't do school!"*

They could see Nicholas smile just a tiny bit.

"And," Mrs. Pidgeon went on, "let's see. Beanie's fable about the bear taught us that being the smallest doesn't make you less of a hero. Remember how the little cub saved his brother?"

Nicholas nodded.

"And Felicia Ann's taught us how to be proud of your color, didn't it?"

Nicholas nodded again. "Even your legth," he said, imitating Felicia Ann.

Mrs. Pidgeon chuckled. "Even your legth," she agreed.

Gooney Bird said, "And Malcolm. He's upset about those triplets. Maybe we could figure out a fable that would help Malcolm with that. Do you have your fable done yet, Nicholas?"

"No."

"Neither do I," said Gooney Bird. "I'm going last. But we could do one together, Nicholas! Would you like that?"

But surprisingly, Nicholas began to cry loudly. "I can't!" he sobbed.

"Why not?" asked Gooney Bird.

"Why not, sweetie?" asked Mrs. Pidgeon, patting his back.

Choking back the sobs, Nicholas told them the reason. "I don't have an animal!" he wailed.

"My goodness," Mrs. Pidgeon said. "That shouldn't be a problem!"

"It has to be an N!" Nicholas wept. "I thought and thought every day, and at night! I tried and tried, but there isn't one! I'm the only one who doesn't have an animal!"

"But what about a—" Then Mrs. Pidgeon hesitated for a long time, thinking, with a puzzled look on her face. "Oh, dear," she said at last. "It *is* a problem. Gooney Bird, what do you think? Can you come up with one?"

Gooney Bird, who felt that taking deep breaths was always helpful in problem-solving, took several deep breaths. She closed her eyes tightly, something she often did while thinking deeply.

Then she opened her eyes and grinned. "YES!" she said. "Got it!"

"What's the answer?" Mrs. Pidgeon asked.

Gooney Bird took Nicholas's hand. She tapped her foot the way Tyrone always did. *"You and me, me and you,"* she chanted. *"Gonna be a secret between us two, 'cuz the teacher dunno and the class dunno, but me and you, we be stars of the show!"*

Gooney Bird grinned. "You'll see, Mrs. Pidgeon," she said. "It'll be the best *suddenly* ever!"

8.

The words BUNNY and TORTOISE had now been added to the list on the board. Ben and Tricia had told the well-known story of the race between the two, the race won by the slow, plodding tortoise (Tricia, the tortoise, had worn old leather gloves, wrinkled and brown, on both hands and both feet) because the foolish hare had been so certain of winning that he had stopped to play and to nap along the way. Ben had attached a cotton ball to the seat of his blue jeans. "I am never ever embarrassed," he had said again, wiggling his behind with its fluffy white puff of a tail.

"I think we all know the moral of that fable," Mrs. Pidgeon said. *"Slow and steady wins the race!"*

Ben hip-hopped back to his desk, and Tricia slid her gloved feet slowly across the wooden floor until she reached hers.

"Me next? Oh, please, me next?" Barry Tuckerman, as usual, had his hand in the air.

"Do we have time for one more today?" Gooney Bird asked.

Mrs. Pidgeon nodded. "Just one," she said.

"Okay, Barry." Gooney Bird pointed to him.

"You can't be a bear!" Beanie said. "I already did BEAR!"

"Or a bunny," added Ben, who was turned around in his seat trying to remove his cotton-ball tail.

Barry Tuckerman came to the front of the room.

"He doesn't have a costume!" Malcolm

called out. "You're supposed to have a costume! Barry doesn't have a —!"

Mrs. Pidgeon put her calm-down arm over Malcolm's shoulders. "Shhh," she said in a low voice. "Barry will explain."

Barry Tuckerman bowed to the class. "I have as much of a costume as Tricia did," he said. "She just had gloves.

"Tyrone only had a pie tin for dinosaur armor. And Ben just had a cotton-ball tail.

"You don't have to have *clothes* for a costume. I have this." He held up something silver and shiny.

The children all peered toward it, trying to see what the small shiny disk was. "It's money!" Keiko said.

"Correct," Barry replied. "It's five cents. It's a nickel."

"Why do you have a nickel?" asked Beanie.

"I'll explain in a minute. Anybody got a nickel?" Barry asked the class. Several chil-

dren reached for their pockets. They shook their heads.

"I have two quarterth," Felicia Ann whispered. "The tooth fairy brought them."

"I have two pennies, in my shoes!" Chelsea announced. "See?" She held one foot up and the children could see that she was wearing loafers with pennies wedged into their slots for decoration.

Mrs. Pidgeon had taken her purse from the desk drawer. "I do, Barry!" she said. "I have a nickel!" She held it up.

"What's on it?" Barry asked. "Look carefully."

Mrs. Pidgeon examined her coin. "Let me see. On one side there's Thomas Jefferson. We all recognize him, don't we?" She pointed to the chart of United States presidents on the wall.

The second-graders nodded and looked at the portrait of the third president.

"He can't be Thomas Jefferson for his fable!" Malcolm shouted. "He can't be, can he? He can't! Because Thomas Jefferson's a guy and for a fable you have to be a—"

"Wait a minute, Malcolm," Mrs. Pidgeon said. "Let me turn my nickel over. Maybe there's a . . . No, it's a house. Here's Jefferson's beautiful big home on the other side. It was called Monticello."

"Big house!" Ben shouted. "B for big house? That's not an animal!"

Tyrone began to rap. *"Good ol' Barry, he be actin' like a fool, 'cuz he don' pay attention when she tellin' the rule . . ."*

"Excuse me!" Barry said loudly, and Tyrone, with an apologetic smile, fell silent.

"Could I see that, please, Mrs. Pidgeon?" Barry asked. She handed him her coin.

"Well," he said, after he had examined it, "there are different kinds of nickels, I guess. And *mine* has a picture of a—"

He went to the board, picked up the chalk, and added his animal to the long list.

BUFFALO, Barry wrote neatly.

"Here is my fable," Barry announced. He opened his paper and read from it, holding his nickel up to the class with his other hand.

The American Buffalo

The correct scientific name for the American buffalo is actually bison. The National Bison Association would like us to use the correct name for this magnificent beast.

Once there had been about sixty million bison in the American West from Canada to Mexico. But by 1893, there were only a little more than three hundred left.

Bison were the center of life for the Native Americans. They provided food, shelter, and clothing. But gradually—

"This isn't a story!" Malcolm called out. "Barry is supposed to be telling a story! It isn't a story about a buffalo!"

"It doesn't have a *suddenly*," Ben added. "It has a *gradually* instead!"

"It is too a story!" Barry replied angrily. "I learned all about it in the encyclopedia!"

Mrs. Pidgeon went to the front of the room, holding up her "Quiet, please" hand toward the class.

"Barry," she said, "you provided us with a real learning experience. I never knew there was a nickel with a buffalo — excuse me, *bison* — on it. And your report is very interesting. One of these days we will have a lesson about doing reports, and we will each have a chance to present one.

"But a report is *nonfiction*."

"What's that mean?" Barry asked. He was looking down at his nickel.

"Well, it means *facts*. And a story is made up, and uses your imagination." Mrs. Pidgeon looked out at the class. "Gooney Bird? Did you have your hand up?"

Gooney Bird nodded. "Barry can make his

buffalo report into a story," she said. "It can be an absolutely true story, and it can have a *suddenly*."

"Barry?" Mrs. Pidgeon said. "Want to try that?"

"I could help you," Gooney Bird told him.

"Well, okay," Barry said. "But it should be about a bison, not a buffalo, because the National Bison Association prefers the correct name."

"*Bithon* thtarts with a B," Felicia Ann pointed out.

Barry nodded. He went to the board, erased the word BUFFALO, and replaced it with BISON.

Gooney Bird Greene went to the front of the class and stood beside Barry. Today she was wearing bib overalls on top of a ruffled blouse, and a pearl necklace.

"It's a good idea to start out with the word *once*," she whispered to Barry.

Barry scrunched his nose. He took a deep breath.

Once over sixty million bison roamed the plains.

Gooney Bird nudged him. "That's nonfiction, still," she said. "Try this." She whispered a sentence to Barry.

Barry began again, using Gooney Bird's opening sentence.

Once a young bison lived with his herd on the plains of North America.

He paused and looked at the class. "Is that okay?" he asked. The second-graders nodded.

"How big was he?" asked Beanie.

"Did he have a name?" asked Chelsea.

"See?" Gooney Bird said to Barry. "They're

getting interested in the character. That's an important thing, with a story."

Barry thought for a moment, and continued.

He didn't have a name. Some people liked to call him Buffalo, but the National Bison Association prefers—

"Wait a minute!" Barry interrupted himself. "I started making a report again, didn't I?"

Gooney Bird nodded. "Start over," she suggested. "We all make mistakes. But you're doing great."

Barry took another deep breath and began his fable again.

Once there was a young bison who lived with his herd. There were about eight hundred of them. They roamed the plains, eating grass and enjoying the sunshine in summer.

In winter, they liked the snow, too, because they had thick fur and were never cold.

"Is that too reporty?" Barry asked Gooney Bird.

"No," she said. "Details are good. I liked knowing about the thick fur because I could picture the bison in my imagination.

"But I'd add a little action to the story now," she said.

Barry nodded and went on.

One day when they were roaming and eating, roaming and eating, hunters with guns crept up on the herd.

"Guns!" said Keiko, and covered her ears. "I don't want to hear any more!"

"Blam!" shouted Malcolm, holding up his hand with his finger aimed like a gun. "Blam! Blam!" Mrs. Pidgeon went to Malcolm's desk and put her calm-down arm across his shoulders.

"Maybe," Gooney Bird said to Barry, "some dialogue would be good now."

Barry frowned. "Bison can't talk," he said.

"In stories they can," Gooney Bird explained. "That's the good thing about stories. Anything can happen."

"Hmmm," Barry said. He was thinking. Then he went on.

"Look!" called the young bison to his herd. "I see hunters coming!"

"Oh, dear!" an older bison said. "If they shoot us, the magnificent bison herds of the western plains may become extinct!"

"Yes," said another old bison, "once there were sixty million of us, but—"

Barry paused. He looked around. Keiko still had her hands over her ears. Malcolm was busy making a cootie-catcher out of paper.

Beanie and Chelsea were beginning a game of tic-tac-toe. Mrs. Pidgeon, back at her desk, was grading their spelling tests.

"Time for a *suddenly*," Gooney Bird whispered to Barry.

"Yes," Barry agreed. He turned back to the class and spoke in a booming voice.

SUDDENLY

The second-graders looked up with interest. Barry grinned and continued.

Suddenly the hunters came riding out of the trees on their horses, shooting their guns, and shot a lot of the bison. Even the young one.

And after that there were practically no bison left in North America.

"That's the end," Barry said. "It's a sad ending."

"Some stories have sad endings," Gooney Bird announced. "It's good to be reminded of that."

Tricia raised her hand. "But what's the *moral?*" she asked.

Barry stood in front of the class with his arms folded across his chest. He thought and thought.

"Guns make a mess of things," he said finally.

9.

"One potato, two potato, three potato, *four*," Gooney Bird chanted, moving back and forth between the clenched fists that Malcolm and Chelsea both held out.

"Out goes Y, O, U," she concluded, and Malcolm scowled, realizing he had lost.

"You'll get your turn next, Malcolm," Gooney Bird reassured him. "Anyway, it's supposed to be ladies before gentlemen.

"Chelsea? Your turn for a fable," Gooney Bird said, as Malcolm, still scowling, went back to his desk. "Malcolm, you'll be next."

Chelsea went up to the front of the class.

"I bet we all can guess what your animal will be," Mrs. Pidgeon said, chuckling, as Chelsea picked up the chalk. "It's so obvious."

Chelsea looked at Mrs. Pidgeon, and then at the class. "No, it isn't," she said. "No one will guess."

Mrs. Pidgeon grinned. "Cluck cluck cluck," she said.

"Cluck cluck cluck?" Chelsea repeated. "Excuse me?"

"Isn't your fable about a chicken?" Mrs. Pidgeon asked.

"Of course not. Who on earth would write a fable about a chicken? Chickens get their heads cut off, and then they get eaten," Chelsea said. She put her hands on her hips. "What kind of fable would *that* be?"

From her desk, Keiko groaned. "Oh, no!" she said. "Head cut off? *Eaten?*"

"Well, my goodness," Mrs. Pidgeon said. "I certainly blundered, didn't I? I thought I knew what you'd choose because of the 'ch' in your name. Chelsea equals chicken."

"Wrong," said Chelsea.

"But what other 'ch' animal is there?" Mrs. Pidgeon asked.

"Chipmunk!" called Beanie.

"Chimpanzee!" called Ben.

"Chinchilla!" called Barry.

"Chinchilla?" Gooney Bird asked. "What on earth is a chinchilla?"

"A small rodent from South America," Barry explained. "It looks like a rabbit, but with big mouselike ears and a squirrel-like tail. It was first introduced into the United States back in —"

He stopped. "I'm giving a report again," he said. "Sorry."

"Have you memorized the encyclopedia, Barry?" Mrs. Pidgeon asked, laughing.

"Almost," Barry said. "Only the A's, B's, and C's, though. I'm working on the D's now."

"And my fable is not about a single one

P THE PANDA
K THE KANGAROO
B BEAR
F FLAMINGO
T&B TORTOISE AN
B BISON
C CHIHUAHUA

322

of those animals," Chelsea announced. "Here is my costume." She took a small leather belt decorated with rhinestones out of her pocket. Carefully she buckled it around her neck.

Then she went to the board and, after checking her paper to be certain her spelling was correct, printed carefully: CHIHUAHUA.

Tyrone made a face as he looked at the word. "Chi-hooah-hooah? I never heard of no chi-hooah-hooah!"

Chelsea explained. "It's a Spanish word. You say it this way: chi-wa-wa."

The second-graders all repeated it. *Chi-wa-wa.*

When she turned and held up her paper to read, Chelsea announced, "The title of my fable is just one word."

Woof

Once there was a teeny tiny dog called a

Chihuahua. He lived in Mexico with a very rich lady.

He slept on a bed made out of one of her old mink coats. He had steak for dinner every single night. He had a collar with diamonds on it.

He was allowed to get on the furniture.

One day, when he was on the sofa, he looked through the window and saw many other dogs playing in the road. They were chasing one another, and biting sticks, and barking at cars.

"Woof!" he said, meaning that he wanted to go out and play with them.

"No, you must stay inside," said the rich lady. "Here. Have a cream puff and a glass of wine."

But the Chihuahua kept looking through the window. "Woof," he said again.

"Woof.

"Woof."

He kept saying it all day long, until the

rich lady was so annoyed that she opened the door to the house and told him, "Okay then, go outside if you want to."

Off he went.

But when the bigger dogs saw him, they did not know what he was. Maybe a cat? Or maybe a chinchilla?

A chinchilla is a small rodent that lives in South America . . .

Chelsea paused. "Oh, dear," she said. "I started making a report."

"That's okay," Gooney Bird told her. "Please go on. Your fable is interesting. It has details, dialogue, and suspense."

So Chelsea continued.

The bigger dogs began to chase the Chihuahua. "Help! Help!" he cried, though in his language it sounded like "Woof! Woof!"

If the rich lady heard him, she paid no attention. She had listened to enough woofs that day. She was playing an opera on her stereo.

The Chihuahua ran as fast as he could on his teeny tiny legs. The bigger dogs kept chasing him. He was never seen again.

"That's the end," Chelsea said to the class.

"But what happened to him?" Beanie asked.

"No one knows," Chelsea explained.

"But a story has to have an ending!" Beanie complained.

"This story leaves you hanging," Gooney Bird told the class. "Some stories do."

"Oh, no!" Keiko wailed. *Hanging?*

"It just means — what's the word, Mrs. Pidgeon?" Gooney Bird asked.

"I think the word would be *ambiguous*," Mrs. Pidgeon said. "Let me look it up." She picked up her dictionary and leafed through the pages of the A's. "Here we are," she said. Then she read aloud, "'Open to many different interpretations.' Yes, Chelsea's story has an ambiguous ending."

The class was silent for a moment. They were all worrying about what might have happened to the Chihuahua.

They looked sad.

"Class," Gooney Bird suggested, "let's think about the moral of the Chihuahua story."

"What color wath the Chihuahua?" Felicia Ann asked shyly.

"Brown," Chelsea replied after she had thought for a minute, "with some spots near his tail."

"Well," Felicia Ann said, "the moral could be *Be proud of your color,* like my flamingo story."

"Yes, it could," Gooney Bird told her.

"I know! I know!" Beanie called, with her hand raised.

"Beanie?" Gooney Bird pointed to her.

"It could be *You don't have to be big or brave.* Like my bear fable."

"It could," said Gooney Bird.

"How about this?" Mrs. Pidgeon said. "Could it be *Sometimes what you already have is the best thing?* Like my panda fable?"

"It could," Gooney Bird said, and all of the second-graders nodded.

"Or my kangaroo story!" Keiko said. *"There's no place like home!"*

"Any one of the morals fits just fine," Gooney Bird pointed out. "Chelsea? What did you have in mind for the moral of your Chihuahua fable?"

Chelsea fingered the leather rhinestone-trimmed collar that was still buckled around her neck. "Here is the moral of my fable," she announced. *"Rich is good. If you have a mink coat, you should stay put."*

The classroom was silent.

Mrs. Pidgeon looked at her watch. "You know what?" she said. "It's lunchtime. And I'm hungry."

"Me, too!" Gooney Bird said. "And guess what! I have an anchovy sandwich today, on date-nut bread. I'll trade half if anyone wants."

10.

No one wanted half of Gooney Bird's sandwich. No one even wanted to sit near Gooney Bird's sandwich.

"Are you sure you wouldn't like some? Last chance," she said. "Keiko?"

"Not I," said Keiko.

"Nicholas?"

"Not I," said Nicholas.

"Barry?"

"Not I," said Barry.

"Tricia?"

"Not I," said Tricia.

The children began to giggle as they went around the table, answering one by one.

Gooney Bird tied her bib. "Well," she said, "in that case, I will eat it all myself." She took a bite and said, "Yum."

"We told the story of the Little Red Hen!" Chelsea said. "Cluck cluck cluck!"

"I can't believe Mrs. Pidgeon thought my fable was going to be about a chicken," she grumbled.

"Here, have a piece of fried chicken," Nicholas said, and handed her a crispy wing from his lunchbox. "Can I have your orange, for a trade?"

Chelsea considered that. "Okay," she said, and handed him her orange. She bit into the chicken wing. "Nobody would eat a Chihuahua," she said. "None of our fable animals are edible."

"Bear is," Beanie pointed out. "Some people eat bear."

"Yuck. Well, not panda, though, or kangaroo, or—what others did we have?"

"Bunny, and tortoise," Tricia said. "People eat those."

"And bison," Barry added. "Bison is a very healthful food. You should eat bisonburgers instead of hamburgers. Less cholesterol."

"Nobody would eat a flamingo," Felicia Ann said. "I think it would make you thick."

"How about T. rex?" asked Ben.

Tyrone, whose mouth was full of tuna fish sandwich, began to wiggle rhythmically in his seat. *"Teee rex, Teee rex,"* he murmured. *"See my muscles flex, if I munch on ol' T. rex . . ."* He lifted his arm and tried to demonstrate the muscle.

"How about Malcolm?" Tyrone asked suddenly, interrupting his own performance. "You didn't do your fable yet, Malcolm. Want me to make you up a rap? What animal you gonna do?"

Malcolm grinned. "Not telling," he said. "Secret. Surprise."

"Well," Gooney Bird pointed out, "your turn comes right after lunch, Malcolm, so it won't be a surprise for long."

"How about Nicholas? Want a rap, Nicholas?" Tyrone was shifting back and forth in his chair, eager to dance.

"I'm going last," Nicholas said.

"You can't! Gooney Bird's going last! She already said so! *The day go fast, and Gooney Bird be last*—"

"Nicholas and I are doing our fable together," Gooney Bird explained. "Look what I have for dessert! A kumquat!" She held it up, and the other children examined it with interest.

"Kumquats are native to China," Barry announced, "although they are now cultivated in the United States. The kumquat tree is slow-growing and compact. Because of their thick

rind, kumquats keep well and are easy to ship long distances."

"I thought you only read up through D in the encyclopedia, Barry," Gooney Bird said.

"I peeked into the K," he explained, "because I'm interested in kites."

"You're amazing." Gooney Bird bit into her kumquat.

"You can't do your fable with Gooney Bird, Nicholas," Ben said. "You're an N and she's a G."

"True," Gooney Bird replied. She grinned at Nicholas and Nicholas grinned back.

"Me and Gooney Bird have a surprise," Nicholas said.

Gooney Bird, imitating Mrs. Pidgeon, held up a grammar finger.

"Gooney Bird and I," Nicholas said. Then, to everyone's surprise, he chanted, *"You and I, me and you, we gotta surprise, oh yes we do . . ."* He collected his crumpled paper napkin and an empty plastic cup. Then he shuffled over to the trashcan, still chanting. Bruno, the Saint Bernard, lay dozing nearby.

"But first," Malcolm announced, rising from the table, "ME! My turn! I'm doing my fable next!"

With Malcolm eagerly leading the way, the second-graders walked back to the classroom. Bruno yawned, stood up slowly, and followed behind, hoping not to miss anything. His antlers were a little tilted.

II.

When the class was settled at their desks and Gooney Bird had announced that it was his turn to present his fable, Malcolm picked up a thick red marker and colored his own nose.

"A clown?" Keiko murmured.

Then Malcolm stood and attached something to his belt, twisting it around to the back. The children all watched, puzzled.

He walked to the front of the room.

Then, with his back turned to the class, he began to write on the board. The children were all still puzzled by the costume: his bright red nose and the sheet of purple construction paper dangling from his belt in the rear.

"Why is your nose red?" called Tricia.

"Why is your backside all purple?" asked Ben.

"Shhhh!" Mrs. Pidgeon said, holding up her quiet-please finger. "Let's see Malcolm's animal, and then maybe we'll understand his costume."

Carefully Malcolm wrote an uppercase M. Then an A. Then an N.

"NO FAIR!" Tyrone called. "He can't be a man!"

"You have to be an animal, Malcolm!" Barry said loudly. "Remember you thought I was Thomas Jefferson and it wasn't an animal? Isn't that right, Mrs. Pidgeon? Isn't that right, Gooney Bird?"

Malcolm had turned around and was looking impatiently at the second-graders.

"Well," Gooney Bird said, "a man is a

mammal. Maybe a fable can be about any mammal."

"But mine wathn't a mammal," Felicia Ann pointed out. "Flamingo ith a bird."

"Neither was mine!" Tricia announced. "I was a tortoise. That's not a mammal."

"You're right." Gooney Bird looked as if she were thinking. "I don't know if there is a rule about fables. If we can have a bird, or a tortoise, or a T. rex, as the main character, maybe we could have a man."

"I wonder what Aesop would say," Mrs. Pidgeon said.

"And anyway, what's that purple thing on your backside, Malcolm?" Chelsea asked. "It's weird. So is your nose."

Malcolm grinned. He wrinkled his nose and wiggled his bottom. Then, when the class grew quiet, he turned and added some more letters on the board.

DRILL

He turned back to the class, wiggled his bot-

tom again, then lifted one arm and scratched with the other. "Oooh, oooh, oooh," Malcolm said, making an odd hooting sound.

"Mandrill!" Gooney Bird announced. "Malcolm is a mandrill!"

"But he's acting like a chimp, or a monkey," Beanie pointed out. Now Malcolm was leaping about, his legs bent, still making the sound.

"A mandrill is a kind of monkey, sort of," Gooney Bird explained. "Like a baboon, I think. I've seen them at the zoo. They're the ones with red noses and—"

"Oh, no!" Keiko squealed. "The ones with the yucky bright blue and pink bottoms! I *hate* those!" She made a face.

Malcolm stopped jumping around. He announced his fable's title.

The Mandrill and Its Young

Once there was a female mandrill who was

expecting a baby. She got very fat. Then one day her baby was born. It was pretty cute. She liked it.

But then, suddenly, she had *another* baby.

And then, suddenly, *another*.

Well. That was pretty surprising. Now she had three mandrill babies. They were very noisy. They wanted to be fed every minute. They made a big mess. They threw things and broke things.

The father mandrill was never home. Sometimes the mother was so nervous and tired that she screamed.

And the worst thing was, the mother mandrill didn't have any time to take care of her older mandrill child.

"Oh, I wish I could get rid of a couple of these babies," she said. "Maybe I can sell them."

She asked all around the jungle, but no one wanted to buy a baby mandrill.

"Well, maybe I can give them away," she thought.

But no one wanted those babies, even as a gift.

She couldn't figure out what to do. She sat on the jungle floor, thinking.

Suddenly one of the babies smiled at her.

Then the next one did.

And then the third. All three baby mandrills were smiling for the first time.

"Hey, look!" the mother said to her older mandrill child. He was up in a tree, hiding, because he hated the babies. But he came down when his mom called.

He looked at the smiles. He reached over and tickled one of the babies. It laughed.

Another one puckered up its mouth and blew him a kiss.

The third one climbed into his lap, curled up, and began to sleep very quietly.

The older mandrill child was surprised at

how much, suddenly, he had begun to like the babies.

"Let's keep them," he said to his mother. "They're cute."

So they did. After that, when the babies cried, the mother mandrill and her older mandrill child just covered their ears. They knew it wouldn't last.

"Oh, I love that fable," Keiko said with a sigh. "It was so sweet."

"Yeth," said Felicia Ann. "Tho thweet."

"Did the babies have purple bums?" asked Tyrone.

Malcolm shrugged. "I guess so," he said. "They were mandrills."

Gooney Bird went to the front of the class. "There is nothing whatsoever wrong with a purple bottom," she said. "Colorful is always good. I'm planning on dyeing part of my hair purple sometime.

"Thank you for your fable, Malcolm. Do you want to tell us the moral?"

"Okay. It's this," Malcolm said. *"Things get better."*

"They do indeed," Mrs. Pidgeon said, smiling. "And it sounds as if things are getting better at your house, Malcolm."

He nodded happily. Then he stopped smiling. "It'll be bad when I get home today, though," he said. "My mom will scream."

"Why is that?" asked Mrs. Pidgeon.

"Because I used an indelible marker on my nose," Malcolm said.

12.

"Who's left?" Mrs. Pidgeon looked around the room. "Just Gooney Bird and Nicholas, I guess. Goodness, we've done a lot of fables!"

"When do we do the parade?" Beanie asked.

"Tomorrow. It's the last day of school before vacation. Have you all saved your costumes? I have my panda vest right here in my desk drawer."

The children all nodded.

"Can I do us a rap for the parade?" Tyrone

asked. "Most parades got a band. We need some kind of music."

"Yes!" the children called. "A rap!"

"Of course," said Mrs. Pidgeon. "But we'll all need to learn it, Tyrone, and we don't have much time."

"Ain't no problem, nuthin' to learn, just follow me and take your turn . . ." Tyrone chanted.

"All right, I guess we can do that," said Mrs. Pidgeon. "We'll have a little practice time before we start the parade." She looked toward the corner of the classroom. "Gooney Bird? Nicholas? Are you ready?"

Gooney Bird and Nicholas had been whispering to each other in the corner by the gerbil cage, planning the presentation of their fable. Now they nodded and came to the front of the room. Nicholas was grinning. It was already hard to remember how sad he had been, how he had stopped eating, and how he had sulked and refused to discuss his fable just a few days before.

They stood side by side and put on their costumes, dark beards that attached by plastic pieces that hooked around their ears.

"They're being Abe Lincoln!" Ben called. "That's not fair!"

"Anyway," Barry pointed out, "Abe Lincoln is A and L! They're supposed to be G and N!"

Gooney Bird held up a quiet-please finger. Eventually the class calmed down, though some of the children were still laughing at the sight of Gooney Bird and Nicholas wearing the dark brown beards, which did not match Gooney Bird's bright red hair, or Nicholas's blond curls, at all.

"We are not Abe Lincoln," Gooney Bird told the class. Her beard wobbled a little as she talked. "We are two animals who live in a large herd on the plains of Africa. Nicholas, will you write our name on the board?"

The list on the board was very long by now. Nicholas had to lean down to add the

final animal at the end of it. Carefully, with the chalk, he made a capital G.

"I *knew* you were going to let Nicholas cheat!" Malcolm called. "He can't be a G animal!"

"Wait, Nicholas," Gooney Bird said. "Do not write any more until I deal with this." She put her hands on her hips and looked sternly at Malcolm.

"Malcolm," she said, "it is very important to have all the information before you come to a conclusion.

"For example," she went on, "if a stranger looked at you, that stranger might think, 'That poor boy has a very bad cold. See how bright pink his nose is.'"

"I don't have a cold," Malcolm argued.

"Of course you don't. The stranger wouldn't have all the information. The stranger wouldn't know that your very pink nose was a leftover mandrill."

"My mom scrubbed it," Malcolm said.

"Nonetheless," Gooney Bird replied, "do you see what I mean, about needing the information?"

"I guess so," Malcolm said. He rubbed his nose.

"Nicholas," Gooney Bird said, "please continue."

Nicholas, holding his beard out of the way with one hand, printed the remaining letters: NU.

"The title of our fable is 'Two Gnus,'" Gooney Bird announced.

"The G is silent," she added.

"If we were doing a story about medieval times," Nicholas said, "I could be a knight, because the K is silent!"

Malcolm frowned. "When does an M get to be silent?" he asked.

"I don't believe an M is ever silent," Gooney Bird said.

"*Malcolm* is never silent," Barry added.

"G's are special," Nicholas said proudly, "and they make my N special."

"Tho thecial," Felicia Ann said with a happy smile.

"Class," Mrs. Pidgeon announced, "maybe after vacation, maybe in January, we will do a whole unit about silent letters, and let's see, homonyms, and synonyms, and—oh yes—*palindromes;* those are especially interesting. But right now, it is time for a fable."

Gooney Bird and Nicholas, side by side, wearing their beards, unfolded their papers and read their fable together.

Two Gnus

Once there were two gnus, a female gnu and a male gnu. They were friends. Both had beards. All gnus, female and male, have beards.

They were part of a large herd and they

moved slowly across the African plains, eating grasses.

Several lions were watching them and making plans for an attack.

"Oh, no!" said Keiko.

"It's okay," Gooney Bird reassured her. "It has a happy ending. Just a little suspense, and a *suddenly*."

The fable continued. Keiko looked nervous but she was quiet.

The lions decided to attack late at night, when it was dark and the gnus were asleep. They planned to carry away several young gnus and have them all for breakfast the next morning.

Gooney Bird looked over at Keiko and whispered, "It's okay. Don't worry."

The lions decided to rest for the early part of the night, so that they would have lots of energy for the big attack. They curled up in a heap in the tall grass and slept. They didn't need an alarm clock. Lions are very good at knowing when to wake up.

The gnus gathered in their herd and prepared to sleep, too. But they were thirsty. It was a time of drought.

"*Drought* has a silent G *and* a silent H," Gooney Bird pointed out to the class. "But we'll talk about those next month."

"Are you *sure* there's no silent M?" Malcolm asked.

"Almost positive," Gooney Bird said. Malcolm scowled.

Suddenly the chief gnu sniffed the air and smelled some water far ahead.

"We really need water," he murmured

softly. "We haven't had water in a long time. I think maybe we should skip tonight's sleep and move forward to get a drink."

He made the special gestures, tossing his head and stamping his foot, that told the entire herd to get moving. And off they went, some of them yawning because they had been almost asleep.

In the middle of the night, at the very darkest time, the lions, who were very rested now and full of energy, woke up. "Time to attack!" the chief lion (a female, by the way. It is always the females who do the hunting. The males are very lazy) announced. "Gnu for breakfast!

"Go!" she said. And the lions leapt out of the tall grass, in attack mode, and dashed to the place where the gnus had been.

But the vast plain was empty. Oh, there was a snake slithering past, and a couple of vultures sitting on the branch of one crummy-looking tree. But the herd of gnus had disappeared. They were far away, having a nice drink of water.

"Bummer," said the lions. "We'll have to have that old leftover zebra for breakfast."

"The end," said Gooney Bird and Nicholas together. They bowed, and the class clapped.

"Good fable!" Mrs. Pidgeon said, getting up from her chair. "And I suppose the moral is something about being watchful and vigilant?"

Gooney Bird and Nicholas shook their heads. "Here's the moral," they said together. *"No gnus is good news."*

13.

"May I march with you?" Mr. Leroy asked.

The children of Mrs. Pidgeon's second grade were lining up in the school hallway on Friday afternoon, the last day of school before the holiday vacation. They all had their bits and pieces of costumes on, and wore nametags revealing the names of their animals. They were wiggling and giggling and shuffling their feet and practicing chanting the rap that Tyrone had prepared for the parade.

"Ask Gooney Bird," Beanie told the principal. "She's in charge."

Gooney Bird Greene was at the head of the parade, wearing her beard and a pair of plaid pajamas. "Well," she said dubiously when Mr. Leroy asked permission to join the group, "we're all animals. You have to be an animal. And," she added, looking at his suit, "you have to have some kind of costume. See Mrs. Pidgeon, in her black shirt and white vest? She's a panda.

"And I'm a gnu," she added, stroking her beard, in case he hadn't already read her nametag or figured it out. "The animal has to begin with the first letter of your name. Gnu has a silent G."

"Yes, I understand," the principal said. "I was in your classroom when Tyrone did the T. rex fable. But I think I can fulfill the requirement. My first name is John: a J. But my middle name is Thomas, so I do have a T, as well. And look! Here's my costume!"

He flipped his necktie, today a bright green one with candy canes on it, so that it dangled in front of his buttoned suit jacket.

"Can I be a tiger? Get it? Tie-ger?" he asked.

Gooney Bird sighed. She put her hands on her hips. "If you were in second grade, Mr. John Thomas Leroy," she told him, "I would tell you that you are trying to bend the rules just a *little* too far. But since you're the principal, I'm going to say yes. You may march."

"Thank you, Gooney Bird." Mr. Leroy turned to find a place in the line.

"Alphabetical!" Gooney Bird called to him. "We're lining up alphabetically. "You'll go back there"—she thought for a moment, then pointed—"after panda and before tortoise.

"I should be there with Nicholas, behind

the flamingo," she explained, "but since I'm
the leader, I'm marching in front."

"Why isn't Nicholas after kangaroo and
mandrill?" Mr. Leroy asked, after he had
looked around.

"Oh, Mr. Leroy, it's a very long story,"
Gooney Bird told him.

"Ready? Let's go!" Gooney Bird called.

"Startin' with a gnu, and we goin' right thru . . ."

the children chanted, along with Mrs. Pidgeon, and, after a moment, Mr. Leroy, who had to listen first to grasp the words, since he had not been there for the rehearsal.

The parade, with Gooney Bird leading, began to shuffle and dance down the hall toward the multipurpose room. The other schoolchildren were there waiting, but Mr. Furillo stood in the hall with his large push broom. *"Goin' right through!"* the custodian joined in, giving his broom a few rhythmic swishes on the tile floor.

Bruno, the Saint Bernard, who had been asleep near the utility closet door, was startled awake. He looked terrified. Quickly he rose to his feet, dropped his tail between his legs, and loped off toward the administration office, where he could hide.

Cute little bear, he got brown hair . . .
Here come the bison, as big as Mike Tyson . . .
Laugh at the bunny if you think he be funny . . .

One by one, alphabetically, they chanted the animal names and the rhyming rap that came so easily to Tyrone. As the parade entered the multipurpose room, the audience of waiting children cheered and clapped. Gooney Bird twirled in a dance step and then gestured to the classes to join in the chant. "Repeat after us!" she called.

Chihuahua, he be teeny, like a piece a
  scaloppine . . .

Chelsea, wearing her rhinestone collar, danced forward as the room full of children repeated the chant about the Chihuahua.

Next Felicia Ann, dressed again in bright pink, twirled while the second-graders chanted, *"Flamingo's legs be brown, she don' wanna put 'em down . . ."* and the rest of the school repeated it. Then,

Got us a gnu, and got us another,
'Cuz the first gnu's a girl and she got her a
  brother . . .

Gooney Bird and Nicholas did a special little gnu dance while the children clapped.

Betcha thought nuthin' would make a rhyme
  with gnu,
But here she be, and her name be kangaroo . . .

Keiko giggled and did a hopping little kangaroo dance. The parade continued shuffling around the room while the entire school clapped in rhythm.

Panda be a babe who be eatin' bamboo,
She be black and white all over and she don't
got no tattoo . . .

Mrs. Pidgeon held out her arms and did a bit of a waltz, but the children were all looking toward the doorway, where Mr. Furillo was standing with his broom. He grinned and held up his right arm so they could see his tattoo of a dagger and snake.

Here come tiger, he be one fierce dude,
He scare everybody wif his attitude . . .

Principal Leroy, who just that morning had made a speech about school budgets to the Watertower Rotary Club at their monthly breakfast meeting, now did a lunging dance across the center of the floor, and growled loudly before he moved back into the parade line and resumed shuffling.

> *Mr. Tortoise be so dumb an' slow,*
> *He dunno when to start and he dunno when*
> *to go . . .*

Tricia, laughing, waved her big leather gloves and did a very slow dance while the children repeated the tortoise chant.

Then, finally, Tyrone moved out of the parade line and all of the children cheered. He turned a somersault, spun in a circle on his back, and then jumped to his feet and started the T. rex part of the rap:

> *Mr. T. rex big but he dunno how to think,*
> *'Cuz his brain be small, and he go extinct . . .*

"He go extinct," repeated all the children and teachers. Tyrone continued:

> *This he the end of our fabulous parade*
> *But there plenty more stories out there to be made*
> *'Cuz ol' Mr. Aesop, he be a winner—*
> *Now we all go home and eat our dinner!*

"Turkey!" said Tyrone later, as the children were putting on their coats. "That's a T. I could do a rap about holiday food!"

"Cranberry sauce! That's a C!" said Chelsea. "Or celery!" She pulled her mittens out of her pockets.

"M for mashed potatoes!" Malcolm announced, zipping his jacket.

"I could be beans!" said Ben as he pulled on his boots.

"Or beets!" suggested Beanie.

"Uh-oh." Tyrone pointed. "Look at Nicholas."

Nicholas, who had been winding his scarf around his neck, was suddenly very still. He looked distressed.

Gooney Bird had removed her beard. She was wearing the sheared-beaver jacket that she sometimes borrowed from her mother. Carefully she wrapped a long scarf around her neck with a flourish. Then she went over to him. "Nicholas," she said sympathetically, "do not even worry about this for one second. We are *not* doing a food rap. We are all going home to enjoy the holidays.

"Right?" She looked around.

"Right," the other children agreed.

"Okay, right," said Tyrone, reluctantly.

"Even though," Gooney Bird said with a grin, "I would be gravy."

LOIS LOWRY is known for her versatility and invention as a writer. She is the author of more than thirty books for young adults. She has received countless honors, among them the Newbery Medal for two of her novels, *Number the Stars* and *The Giver,* the first novel in the Giver Quartet. Ms. Lowry now divides her time between Cambridge, Massachusetts, and an 1840s farmhouse in Maine. To learn more about Lois Lowry visit her website, **www.loislowry.com.**